BODY ART

BODY ART

A THRILLER

JORDAN CASTILLO PRICE

jcpbooks.com

Print edition published in the United States
in 2016 by JCP Books.
www.jcpbooks.com

First Standalone Print Edition

ISBN-13 978-1-935540-85-4

Cover art by Jordan Castillo Price

Audio edition available

Chapter One

Wanted:
Driver, Red Wing Island. Must speak English and have
current Michigan chauffeur license. Room, board, and
stipend provided. Single gentleman over 35 preferred.
Smokers need not apply.

Was it still legal to discriminate against smokers? I wasn't sure, but I thought it might give
me an edge. I read the ad through again. I had a
brand-spanking-new piece of plastic that enti-
tled me to drive a cab, bus, or limousine. I was
also flat broke, in debt up to my eyeballs, and
I sorely needed somewhere to stay. Oh, and I
spoke English too.

I'd followed the *Guide to Gainful Employment* to
a tee. New haircut. New shirt. New slacks. New
tie—new to me, anyway. Even polished my shoes
for the first time in my life. The final tip, according to the Guide, was to be sure to address the
interviewer by name, using a mnemonic device,

if necessary, to do it.

It hadn't mentioned what to do if there were two interviewers. Damn.

Two women turned up for the interview in the back office of the employment agency. There was an old one—eighties, I'd guess—and a younger one, a handful of years older than me. Maybe forty or so. A stocky, sturdy forty, with hair cropped short and gray at the temples. No makeup. The daughter? Maybe. She didn't look like an accountant or a lawyer, that's for sure. She glanced down at her paper, and asked me, "If a drawbridge does not have a signal light or attendant, how many feet away must you stop and check if the draw is closed?"

That was just on my test. "Fifty."

I'd been so excited to know the answer to that one that I'd leaned forward and allowed my tie to slide out of place. The missing button midway down the shirt gaped. I hadn't noticed it at the thrift store. I'd just been glad to find a dress shirt for less than three bucks that didn't need to be ironed. I covered the buttonhole with the tie. And then I realized the gesture had caused my sleeve to ride up and show a glimpse of my ink. Damn it. Maybe they hadn't noticed. They were looking me in the face, weren't they? Both of them? I hoped so—the kind of hope where your stomach twists up and squeezes itself 'til you're sick. Because I really, really needed that job.

The old woman, Mrs. White, which was easy to remember—white hair, white pearls, Mrs. White—reached over and tapped the other one on the forearm. My guts twisted against themselves harder. She'd seen. And decided I wasn't the sort of man she wanted living under her roof.

I couldn't dream up a neat mnemonic trick for the younger woman, Ms. Friedman, but I figured I could handle two names. She nodded vaguely and shuffled her questionnaire. "Do you have any family nearby, Mr. Carlucci?"

I itched to tell her to call me Ray, since I was only "Mr. Carlucci" to the legions of bill collectors I'd been picking off my sorry hide over the last year, but I figured it wasn't my place to dictate who was called what during the interview. "Parents in Florida."

Mrs. White spoke up. "Any wife? Children?"

And then I remembered the ad. Single gentleman preferred. Which seemed about as politically incorrect as specifying a nonsmoker. "No. Never married. No kids."

Queer as the day is long, actually. But right now? A single gentleman. It made me sound a lot ritzier than I was, but I supposed I fit the bill.

"On your application," said Friedman, "you wrote down 'business owner' as your last job. What was that?"

An answer I'd prepared for. "Custom art." Because tattoo parlor didn't have quite the same ring.

"And you list the reason for leaving as financial."

"That's right."

I did my best to sound mild, but inwardly, I steeled myself against the possibility that they'd poke at some old wounds that hadn't quite closed yet. And I reminded myself to take it like a man, sit up straight, and make sure that damn buttonhole didn't show.

Friedman said, "I had a catering business before." Her gaze went inward, just for a second. "So much work—sixty, seventy-hour weeks. And then the check for a wedding bounced…." She spread her fingers in a "poof" gesture. And I looked at her, really looked at her, and nodded again. Because I could tell she understood that sometimes we fail—grandly, spectacularly—through no fault of our own. It gave me hope.

I didn't feel like I could afford to cling to that hope, though. I nodded.

Friedman's cheeks flushed. "Those are all the questions I have." She turned toward Mrs. White. "You?"

White leaned forward and squinted. Her eyes had the cloudy, watery cast of age. "He looks fit. How tall are you?"

"Six-three," I said. Not one of the interviews I'd sat through in the past several months had asked me if I had kids or how tall I was.

None of them had called me back afterward, either. Until this one.

Chapter Two

The cab ride to Red Wing Island took every last cent I had. That was good, I told myself. The farther away my new digs were from Traverse City and my gutted shop, or the nearby town where Johnny and I had shared a rented house on a street full of overpriced boutiques, the better. The bill collectors had started to get nasty. One of them had threatened to have the local police show up on my doorstep. I hadn't mentioned that to the guy who'd been putting me up. It was bad enough I'd taken over his TV room.

Red Wing Island was maybe fifteen minutes outside town, but it was out in the middle of so much wilderness that it seemed incredibly far away. And incredibly far away was just what I needed.

Even as I watched the meter click forward, impossibly fast, every now and then a startling shock of red or gold would draw my eyes away from the ever-rising number and up to the spectacular trees. It was autumn, and the coast of Lake Huron bustled with a surge of yachters and tourists who would pack it all in once the leaves dropped and the snow started to fall.

The car bumped over a precarious one-lane wooden bridge, then tunneled beneath a canopy of maples that obliterated the sky. The road on Red Wing was rippled and cracked where the roots of the trees had heaved up out of the sandy soil beneath the asphalt with each winter freeze and spring thaw. We passed by a number of bright mailboxes, cutesy folk art things with shingles that hung off the bottom announcing the name of the owners, the Hunt's or the Smith's. I wondered if all sidewalk-fair woodburners had excessive apostrophes they needed to get rid of, or if it was just their way of getting back at people rich enough to own multiple homes and stupid enough not to know how to pluralize their own names.

I scoped out the driveways as best I could, but didn't spot anything that would suggest that the summer residents were still there: smoking fireplaces, dogs, cars, trash.

And then one of the dark recesses between the tree trunks shifted, and I saw that there was life on the island after all. A dark-haired guy dressed all in black stared up into the trees, then reached out and chalked a circle on one of the tree trunks just as the cab passed him by. He didn't strike me as a forester checking for emerald ash borers or Dutch elm disease. Foresters wore reflective orange jackets and Carhartt boots. This guy had hair down to his shoulders and was decked out in a duster worthy of The Matrix.

I craned my neck and tried to get a better look at him through the rear window, but we rounded a curve, and the tree line swallowed him. A few more twists and turns, and the cab pulled up in front of a gate a few yards in from the road.

"Is this it?" I checked the number. That was it. I peered through the trees, blood red maples, and black locusts with dangling brown pods, and tried to make out the shape of the building. It was white, I saw, and it peeked through the tree trunks in areas absurdly far away from one another, the width of three normal-sized houses stacked side by side.

Well, what else did I expect? People in modestly sized houses didn't hire servants.

The gates were closed. I glanced at the meter yet again as the driver got out to open them, and I nearly had a stroke. I couldn't afford the trip up the quarter-mile driveway.

I hopped out and jogged up to the half-open gate. "Here." I slapped money into his hand. "Leave me off here. It's all I've got."

The cabbie frowned down at the money with suspicion in his eyes as he counted it. "All right," he said. No doubt he was pissed off that he wasn't getting a tip. But he couldn't very well hold my luggage hostage for not tipping. He unloaded the trunk, slammed it shut harder than he had to, and drove off without a word.

I dragged my luggage, two by two, inside the gate. Given the scarcity of traffic on the island, it was unlikely that the guy chalking the trees was now lying in wait to steal my luggage, but old habits died hard. Everything I owned was in those six mismatched suitcases and single garment bag. I wasn't about to leave them out on the road.

I went to the main house and spent a good ten minutes trying to figure out which door to use, finally settled on one with a pair of muddy boots outside it in back. There was no bell. I knocked, and Friedman answered. She wore a long white apron spattered with partially bleached stains, loose paisley pants, and clogs. She stuck her head out the door and looked around. "Where's your car?"

"I cabbed it," I told her. She looked confused. "I assumed I'd be using the company car for Mrs. White."

"Oh...sure. Of course. It's just that it's a heck of a long walk between Red Wing and anywhere else. I don't know if she'll want you borrowing the Town Car."

"It's fine. If I need to go off the island, I'll call a cab." Hopefully the driver who'd just let me off wouldn't complain too thoroughly to the rest of his fleet.

"That's way too expensive. You could always borrow mine, if you know how to drive a stick." She laughed. "Well, of course you do, you're a professional driver."

She didn't make it sound half-bad; the way she put it, you'd think I drove in NASCAR. "My bags are by the gate. If you just show me where to put them...."

"Your apartment's above the garage. Mr. and Mrs. are old-fashioned that way." Not Mr. and Mrs. *White*. Just Mr. and Mrs. "Raymond? I can call you that, can't I?"

"Ray," I said. I was staring over my shoulder because my eyes prickled at the thought of something as simple as having my own place again, after spending months rotating through the couches of each of my remaining friends—in exchange for tattoos, of course. Until I finally had to choose between selling my gear and eating.

"Ray. I'm Marnie."

I nodded but kept my head still turned away.

"Technically, I'm just the cook. But the housekeeper, Melita—she's been here three years longer than me—only wants to get her job done and watch soap operas. So I've been the go-to person ever since Mr.'s Alzheimer's took a nosedive, and Mrs. started spending all her time taking care of him. So if you have any questions...you can come to…. Hey, are you all right?"

I turned my back to her and pinched the bridge of my nose. "Yeah. I'll let you know when I've got all my bags upstairs."

"It's a long haul to the gate," she said. "Why don't I bring my car around…?"

I'd already gone a few yards down the path. I gave Marnie a forget-about-it wave without turning around, and she didn't pursue it. She seemed to understand that I needed a few minutes to myself more than I needed a hand with my luggage.

The apartment over the garage smelled slightly of stale bleach and mothballs. It consisted of three rooms: a bathroom, a bedroom, and an everything-else room with a sink, dorm fridge, microwave, and coffeepot on one end, a couch and a TV on the other. I tried to think of them as *my* couch, *my* coffeepot, in the same casual way that I used to think about *my* shop, *my* custom Ford Explorer, *my* boyfriend. And I found I couldn't do it anymore. It felt like a hotel room, with me just passing through.

I changed shirts, since I'd sweated through the first one carrying all that luggage, and hoped there was somewhere I could do a load of laundry, since I only had two dress shirts to my name— one of them now with a button held on by dental floss, a button that almost matched the others, but not quite.

Asking about the laundry would be a good enough lead-in for me to talk to Marnie without having to explain what my silent treatment by the door had been about, anyway...if I could figure out a way to say I'd gotten choked up at the thought of having my own place again, without coming right out and saying it. Maybe I could tell her there'd been something in my eye. I jogged down the stairs two at a time and noticed that they didn't sound hollow like I would've expected. They were as solid and sturdy as interior-grade stairs. Classy.

I was almost at my usual level of confidence and swagger as I stepped out of that garage, or close enough to it that I'd fool a stranger, anyway. I had a roof over my head and a bed to sleep in, and I was miles away from the shop, the gutted hull that was left of it after Johnny's three-card monte and all the repo men that showed up in its wake. Heartless bastards, running their hands over my chairs, my display cases....

My foot hit something slick and shot out from under me. I staggered and hopped and barely caught myself from going down hard. Good thing. The cobblestone was spattered with blood.

"Holy...."

Blood and feathers. A mangled gull was smeared across the path that connected the garage to the house. It stank of bird and blood, but mostly fish. I rubbed my shoe against the grass. Good thing I hadn't fallen on my ass. My other pairs of pants were all holey jeans that were fine for a day at the shop, not so fine for my first day on the job at a sprawling estate.

I walked the rest of the way through the grass, dragging my feet. Bits of gore and a few feathers managed to stick despite my best efforts. Eventually, I took the damn shoe off so I could rinse it down inside, and when Marnie opened the door, I had a much more distracting conversation starter in my hand than I could ever have hoped for. "A bird exploded outside my front door, and now I need to wash off my shoe."

She looked at me big-eyed for a long, hard second. And then she burst out laughing.

Chapter Three

Marnie was less flashy than the old crowd I hung around with in Traverse City, and in fact was dowdy enough that she looked like she could have been "mom" to some of the younger kids. But what good had all those pretty, pretty peacocks been to me when Johnny was funneling my business loan payments into Oxy and Jack? Someone must have known. Me? I put in twelve-hour days more often than not, rolled into bed sore and sandy-eyed. But our friends? Some of them *had* to have known.

Fuck. He'd probably been supporting their habits too.

And so Marnie, with her graying hair and her conservatively single-pierced ears and her pale, uninked skin and her robust laugh that threatened to burst out of her at the slightest provocation—I liked her. A lot.

"We don't have to sit here and watch the laundry spin," she told me. "It's not going anywhere."

"Good to know." The seagull cleanup had been worse than I'd expected. At least now I knew where the hose was. I figured I could give the Town Car a good scrub to earn my keep if Mrs. White didn't need to go anywhere that night. And I thought that maybe, blood and guts aside, this whole servant gig might not really be all that bad.

And then a bell in the kitchen rang. Tink-a-tink, like someone making a toast with coffee mugs. We barely heard it over the sound of the dryer "That's Mrs.," Marnie said. She pushed a button on an intercom on the countertop. "What's up?"

A jumble of noises came from the other end. Zombie movie, I thought. Moaning, with frantic talking over the top. "He's had an accident."

I imagined some brittle old guy falling and shattering, but the wince Marnie gave seemed more inconvenienced than frightened. "I'll be right up. And Raymond's here, so we'll have some help." She turned off the intercom and looked at me. "It's shower time."

"Oh. That kind of accident."

"You got it. Mr. will be happy to have a man getting him into the tub again—as far gone as he is, he's still shy about strange women seeing him naked, and it takes both of us to clean him up. We have this harness that's supposed to bear his weight, but it's too tight of a squeeze to maneuver him into the tub...."

"Marnie." She'd been speaking quickly and

overly bright, and when I stopped her, the silence was pronounced. "I'm not a nurse. I don't know how to handle someone with Alzheimer's."

"When you filled out your application, you said you had no physical limitations. Is that true? Do you have a bum back or trick knee that'll stop you from helping a hundred-and-sixty-pound man in the shower?"

"Well, no, but...."

"Then come upstairs and meet him." She looped her arm through mine. "He was a really fun guy a couple of years ago. That probably won't come through right now, not tonight, but once you've been here a while, I think you'll see it."

We passed a short, dark woman of about fifty in the hallway. She was dark-skinned, maybe Hispanic, maybe Mediterranean. She carried a plastic laundry basket in front of her with her arms stretched as far forward as they could reach. When I caught a whiff of the soiled clothing inside, I guessed why.

"Melita, this is Ray, the new driver."

Melita glanced at me. "Well, I hope you'll stick around longer than the last one."

"She's crabby because they interrupted her TV show," Marnie whispered, once Melita was out of earshot. "She's not exactly a barrel of monkeys the rest of the time either. But she's really sharp, really detailed."

I wouldn't be a barrel of monkeys either if it

was my job to clean up other people's shit.

Mr. White was a few inches shorter than me, about ten years older than my father, and as sinewy as a bantamweight boxer. That first time I met him, he was wearing a blue oxford dress shirt, a green and gray striped towel around his waist, and a pair of monogrammed leather slippers. His jaw was clenched shut tight, and he was doing his damnedest to shove Mrs. White away from him.

"Ray is here," said Marnie. I wished she could take it back. I suddenly wanted to be anywhere but there.

"He's had an accident," Mrs. White said. "He's upset."

"Hey, Mr.," Marnie said. "This is Ray—you gave him a job. How about you let him help you get cleaned up?"

Did Marnie possess the uncanny ability to dig straight into my mind and stab my pride? Maybe I hadn't signed up to see octogenarians naked—but it was true, the Whites had given me a shot at picking myself back up again when no one else would.

I tried to smile, but it felt forced. The best expression I could pull off was "brisk," so I aimed for that. "Hello, Mr. White. Thank you for the opportunity. It's my first day here, so I'd appreciate it if you showed me the ropes...."

I don't know if Mr. White understood me,

exactly. He didn't speak. But he stopped struggling, and he allowed Mrs. White to place his rigid arm in mine so I could lead him to the bathroom.

A look passed between Marnie and Mrs. White. Like me, neither of them was exactly beaming. All any of us could muster, it seemed, was a sense of grim satisfaction.

I'd be lying if I said that the initial spark of connection between Mr. White and me foreshadowed the relationship to come. Dementia had its hooks too deep in him for that. Still, he did seem calm as I helped his wife unbutton his shirt—a better shirt than either of the ones I currently owned, I noted, with no stains and all its buttons. Mrs. White ran the shower and made sure the water wasn't hot enough to scald him. "You'll get wet," she told me. "I'm sorry."

She stared at me a half a beat longer than I would've expected. I'm guessing the apology was in regard to more than just the soaking I was about to receive.

The room was warm and the water barely more than tepid. "You probably want to take off your shoes and socks," Mrs. White suggested. "Bare feet have a better grip on the tub."

"You want me...in there?"

"To help him onto the seat and back off again. The showerhead is detachable, but...."

I looked at the white plastic bench that spanned

the shower. She was right. I would have better control if I got in behind it, especially barefoot. But the top of my right foot was covered by the trailing edge of the barbed wire tat that took up most of my right leg. I kicked off my dress shoes, since they were the only pair I had, but I left my socks on. "Let's do this," I said, and I took Mr. White by the arm while his wife guided his leading foot over the edge of the tub.

Mrs. White did her best to direct the spray only at him, but I was soaked through within the first five minutes. "All right, Edgar," she said. "Stand up. Almost done."

Between the two of us, we stood him up and nudged him around to face me. I didn't want to look him in the eye, but what else could I do? His fate and mine had conspired to bring us together this way, both of us stripped of most of the things by which we'd once defined ourselves, and both of us covered in our own shit.

My shit was metaphorical. It couldn't be washed away so easily.

And so I did look Mr. White in the eye, and I said, "We're almost done." The stream of water hit him as his wife cleaned away the dregs of the "accident," and he reached out to steady himself on my arm. I wasn't prepared for the strength in those thin, wrinkled fingers. They dug into my forearm like a vise. I kept my expression mild despite the pain. Like I'd just said, we were almost done.

Mrs. White cut the water and draped a terry-cloth robe around Mr. White's shoulders. "Thank you, Ray," she said. "That was the easiest shower we've had since Gene left." I planted one wet-socked foot on the bath mat outside the tub and steadied Mr. White while she maneuvered his legs over the edge.

"This would be a lot less work in a walk-in shower," I said. And a lot less likely to end with Mr. White cracking his head open on the porcelain. Together, we guided him back into the master bedroom.

"It was easier for him just a few weeks ago. I had no idea it would get this...." Mrs. White stopped speaking. She was looking at my arm so strangely, I wondered if her husband had torn my shirt when he grabbed me.

The sleeve of my soaked shirt clung to my arm. I could see straight through the wet fabric to the flaming skull on my forearm. I was so drenched that all the ink on my upper body showed, the Japanese dragon, the tribal shoulder piece, the cheesy flash tiger and eight ball with sentimental value, and the spiderwebs on my elbows. Everything that wasn't covered by my undershirt stood out plain as day.

"So many of the contractors are only seasonal," Mrs. White said, as if the abrupt pause had never happened. "They get more work down south over the winter. I've put in some calls, but I haven't heard back yet."

"Right," I said. When life sideswipes you, it doesn't call ahead and make an appointment. "I'm sure we'll manage 'til they get around to calling you back."

Chapter Four

By the time I finally crawled into bed, I ached from top to bottom from wrestling with Mr. White. I wondered if, by some perverse twist of logic, my body would be worse off in the morning for having slept in an actual bed, rather than a couch, or a futon, or an air mattress with a slow leak that was impossible to locate.

I stripped down to my boxers and got under the covers. They'd been through the wash prior to my arrival. They smelled like detergent and dryer sheets.

Clean laundry must be one of those scents that triggers the release of a cocktail of feel-good neurotransmitters. Within moments I was drifting off, finger-shaped bruises, wrenched shoulder, strange bed, and all.

A noise startled me from sleep, just as I was falling hard and fast. I sat up and shook off the sickening lurch of sudden wakefulness at the cusp of dreaming. The house smelled wrong, of someplace that had been vacant—just a couple of weeks, but long enough to develop the sour stink of disuse. It sounded wrong too, surrounded by the continuous drone of cicadas and crickets and the dry friction of leaves on the roof as the wind made the branches scour the shingles.

Another noise rose from the layered background of insects and flora: a sharp crunch, like something breaking.

I flipped on the bedside light, dug out some jeans and a T-shirt that wouldn't look any the worse for wear if I snagged them on the undergrowth, unearthed my leather jacket and biker boots from the heaviest suitcase, and went outside for a look.

The first startling thing was that the moon was bright. Maybe I'd seen it, or something like it, in paintings or in films. But there were no streetlights on Red Wing Island to taint the glow of the stars. The porch light that had lit my way from the main house to the garage was off. And since all of the neighbors had migrated back to their winter homes, the houses all around the estate were dark too.

I had never seen the moon so bright.

I stared up at it as if I'd never seen the moon, period. It was so intensely luminous, that maybe I never had, not really.

Another loud crack from the tree line startled me out of my moongazing as effectively as it had pulled me from the oblivion of sleep. I wished I had a flashlight. I could probably find one in the garage or the car, if I knew where to look, but I didn't. Still, I needed to see for myself what was going bump in the night if I ever hoped to get to sleep. I took a few steps toward the trees and listened. Cicadas droned louder than I would've ever thought possible, louder still if you actually tuned in to them and tried to imagine where that wall of noise might actually be coming from.

A few more steps, and I was at the tree line. The wooded area wasn't large, maybe ten yards deep, and beyond that, more moonlight, bright through the black vertical slashes of the tree trunks. I eased forward, feeling for rocks and fallen branches with my boots as I half shuffled, half walked. I was almost through the trees when I heard the sound again.

Crrack.

I squatted and groped. My fingers brushed fallen leaves and points of cool sliminess, probably slugs. I flicked them away, found a branch with the diameter of a Louisville Slugger TPX, and hefted it. Longer than a TPX. Awkward. But better than nothing.

I inched to the clearing with my heart in my throat, dead sure that every shuffle, every tentative step, had sent a telltale crackle broadcasting my presence throughout the island. A twig snapped. I froze. The drone around me continued, unaffected. I took another few steps forward, now moving even slower, and as I came to the edge of a clearing, I saw him.

A man.

More accurately, the guy in black from the side of the road. Or if you wanted to split hairs, his silhouette. He hung from the lowest branch of a tree, maybe seven feet off the ground, arms and legs locked around the tree limb. His long coat, long hair—and now a long scarf that he'd added to his ensemble—dangled beneath him. He inched forward and caught a smaller branch with one hand. Moonlight glinted off metal as he pulled a blade from the grip of his teeth. He clenched hard with his legs and started to saw at the smaller branch. When he'd sawed about half-way through, he bent the branch back upon itself.

Craack.

"What are you doing?" I called.

His silhouette shifted as he faced me. He tucked the knife away, let go with his legs, hung for a second by his hands, and then dropped. The leaves below him gave off a rumpled sigh.

He trailed the branch he'd cut behind him as he crossed the clearing. It dragged through the fallen leaves with a *shish-shish-shish*. He walked like a runway model, all attitude and hips. And when he stopped in front of me and tossed his dark hair over his shoulder so he could get a look at me, I forgot how to breathe. He was breathtaking, in a wasted sort of way. All soulful eyes and long sideburns and five o'clock shadow.

"What are you doing?" I said a second time. Because what else could I say? *Don't tell me you're an overbooked gardener?* Or, *it's late?* Or, *what's it gonna take to get you out of all those clothes?*

"I'd tell you," he said. "But then you'd think I'm crazy."

I was forming a fast opinion of him, all right, but *crazy* wasn't the word that sprang to mind. Hot. That was more like it. Because straight men didn't walk that way, and no matter how much I told myself not to notice, my eyes kept raking him up and down. "Try me."

A full smile then, wide enough that moonlight glinted, bluish, off his teeth. His teeth had character. Not quite straight, a hairline gap between the front two. Very white.

"What am I doing? Trying to make sense of the world. Just like everybody else."

He pivoted on one foot, stepped over the branch, and started walking back the way he'd come. I watched the silhouette of his back and tried to decide if he was real or just a really vivid dream induced by the scent of mothballs and bleach.

He paused halfway across the clearing and looked back at me. "Aren't you curious?" he said.

The thought of waking up in my garage

apartment the next morning to a day of cleaning up blood and shit, and if I was lucky, driving Mrs. White to an ophthalmologist's appointment, without ever knowing what the mystery man in the trees was actually doing...that really didn't seem like an option. I followed.

He walked quickly, sure-footed in the dark. I walked right behind him in the path he created by dragging his branch. He strode up to a tripod of tree branches tethered at the top in a crude tepee shape, and he propped the branch he was dragging against the existing structure. "Give me a hand, and I'll show you," he said.

He kicked a couple of the branches apart and centered the new branch between them. "Hold this." He grabbed me by the wrist and guided my hand to the hub where the four branches met, then pulled a ball of twine from his pocket and wrapped the joint. He drew his knife, cut the twine, then tucked the knife away again.

"My mother told me never to talk to strange men with knives," I said.

"Good thing your mother's not here." He stepped back with his hands on his hips and scrutinized his tepee. "Unless you're a White." He cocked his head toward the estate. "Is that where you came from?"

"Yeah. But I'm not family. I just work there."

"Doing what?" he said, skeptical. Which

irritated me.

"Driver." My tone of voice said, *Got a problem with that?*

He turned to face me and squinted at me in the moonlight. "But they just got a new driver a couple of months ago—and you're not him. This other guy was blond. Kinda dumpy."

"I don't know why he quit. I guess it was sudden."

"Hmph. You got a name?"

"Ray."

"Hello, Ray. I'm Anton, the family pariah who only has a roof over his head due to the kindness of his sister's heart." He pointed somewhere among the trees. "That's Diane's summer home. She ever so generously lets me stay in the guesthouse. And she locks me in if she's entertaining, so I can't frighten her guests."

"How does one go about becoming an pariah?" I asked. "It sounds like an interesting career move."

"That's true. There's never a dull moment in the we-all-think-you're-crazy profession."

Anton and I stared at the tepee together in silence for a long moment. And then I said, "Are you?"

"What?"

"Crazy. Because last I heard, building wigwams by the light of the full moon didn't rank real high in the 'sane' category."

"That reads as a wigwam to you?" He stepped back a few paces and took in the whole structure with a critical glance. "It's a pyramid. Obviously."

"My mistake."

Anton circled his branch pyramid, then nodded and kicked one of the limbs into position. "You have to get everything right, the position, the angle, or else it won't work."

"It does something?"

He backed up a few steps and stood beside me, appraising his handiwork. "We'll see. It's a test."

"Like the circles you were chalking on the trees by the road."

"Exactly." He wiped his hands on the front of his long coat, then shifted topics as if we'd been talking about something so obvious and mundane it required no explanation at all. "What bothers me is that I didn't know the old driver was gone. Marnie should've told me. How long ago did you say he left?"

"I didn't. I think it was about a week ago. Maybe ten days."

He clucked his tongue. "That means my count was off for a whole week."

He circled his stick pyramid again, and a little voice inside me suggested that I should probably back away. Now. I told my caution to go to hell. Where had it been when Johnny was robbing me blind? It was no wonder my caution was currently in the doghouse. "What's this count?" I said. "Or can't you explain that to me either?"

He turned from his pyramid and looked at me,

surprised. "Don't mock me."

"I'm not."

He crossed his arms over his chest, glanced back at the pyramid, took a deep breath, and began. "Me. Marnie. Mr. and Mrs. White—the guy never leaves the house—Gene, the driver—now you, and not Gene, and the housekeeper. I always forget her name."

"Melita."

"Right. Only us. Six. If we're all accounted for, then who's wandering the island at night?"

I felt a chill that wasn't entirely from the cold. "What do you mean? Did you see someone or just hear them? Maybe it's an animal."

"I can tell the difference between an animal's footsteps and a human's. Especially when the leaves are this dry."

"So you're going by sound."

Anton nodded.

"It could be anything. The wind. Or some homeless guy who walked over the bridge looking for a summer home to flop in."

"No bums, not around here. Every property on the island is wired up to a security outfit on the mainland, just over the bridge and fifteen miles down the road. You so much as rap on a window, you've got a deputy on your doorstep in half an hour." He toed some leaves out of the way, dislodged a stone from the ground, and rocked it with the sole of his combat boot. "I should know.

Diane's got her main house rigged so I can't even go in to grab a coffee filter."

"She got a reason to worry?" I said. Because it occurred to me that maybe I had a "type," and maybe that type was the sort of guy who'd sell his elderly mother's hearing aid for his next fix.

I'd expected Anton to take offense—and in fact, I had a suspicion that I'd been trying to pinch something off before it even had a chance to grow—but instead I caught the glint of moonlight off his teeth as he cracked a grin. "It's not my fault she's got such atrocious taste. That redecorating jag last April? I am never gonna live that down."

Anton took a few more steps back, planted his hands on his hips, and looked at his pyramid. "Too steep. Proportion's all wrong. I'll need to spread out the base. Here. Hold that side for me."

I held the limb he pointed out while he went around the other side and adjusted the angle. The stick pyramid gave rustling protests each time he repositioned a leg. "So once you've got the angle just so. What then?"

"I have no idea. I told you. It's an experiment." He approached me around the back of the structure and grabbed the branch I'd been steadying. "C'mon, pull it out. Think Great Pyramid of Giza. That's the shape we're aiming for."

I realized I had no idea what sorts of angles the sides of the Pyramid of Giza formed. "Is that the same shape as the pyramid on the back of the dollar bill?"

Anton stopped pulling on the branch and stared.

"The one with the floating eye over it?" I said. Because his silence was a little bit on the creepy side.

"The eye," he said. "What's that. Masonic? Rosicrucian?"

"I have no ide—"

Anton sprinted off so fast, I swore someone was chasing him. Twigs snapped and leaves crackled, but he made surprisingly little noise for a guy running through a foot of dried foliage in near darkness. "Wait," I called after him. "Where're you going?"

About thirty yards away from me he stopped and turned, a silhouette in a long black coat. "I've gotta look this up. Don't wait up for me. I'm in the zone."

I'll say. The Twilight Zone. A whirl of his coat and a couple minutes of receding leaf rustles, and he was gone.

Chapter Five

"Ray? Are you awake yet?"

I had a moment of "where am I?" panic, followed by cascade of images—Mr. White in the shower; the empty apartment that smelled like bleach and felt like abandonment; Anton hanging from the tree branch with long hair, coat and scarf dangling beneath him.

"Yeah. I'm awake." I glanced in the direction of Marnie's canned voice. I had my very own intercom. There was a digital clock next to the speaker. It was after ten. Then I looked at the intercom itself. There was a button to press to talk. "I'm awake," I repeated, once I'd pressed it. "Was I supposed to be there at nine or something?"

"I'll let you know ahead of time if we'll ever need you that early. Breakfast is on. After that, I thought I'd go over the job and then show you around the island."

I showered, dressed in my second shirt and my slightly damp pants, and made my way to the kitchen without skating partway there on an exploded seagull.

Breakfast was fresh honeydew melon, bran muffins, and an egg white frittata. It could've used some bacon, but I wasn't about to complain. "I'm accustomed to putting in long hours," I said as Marnie loaded the dishwasher. "But the live-in thing's new to me. What's the routine?"

"The staff is salaried. Theoretically, that means our salaries are based on a fifty-hour work week minus living expenses." She shrugged. "Then again, last night was a good example of how things can crop up."

Marnie wiped her hands on a towel that hung from the apron tie at her waist, and found a small stack of papers. "Here it is in black and white. I think they'll let you take the Town Car out once they've known you for a while, but like I said, you can borrow mine if you need to. Let me know if you're going off the island, so that I'm available in case Mr. needs anything."

Like a trip to the emergency room. She didn't need to spell it out.

"We can negotiate nights off between us. If you want Friday and Saturday, be my guest. I hate the bar scene, I'm not seeing anyone right now, and I have no plans to put myself on the market."

"Ouch."

Marnie wiped her hands on her towel again, even though they were already clean. "I stopped just short of saying that men are pigs. Did you read my mind?"

"Must have. And I agree—but then one comes along and gives you a look, and it's all downhill from there."

She opened her mouth to reply and then broke into a surprised smile. "You're into guys." She shook her head. "I never would've guessed."

I stood, slid my melon rinds into the trash, and loaded my plate into the dishwasher. "Is that supposed to be a compliment?" I teased.

She'd crossed her arms over her chest and was giving me the once-over. "What about the tattoos?"

"Mrs. White told you about that, huh? Gay guys are allowed to have them too, you know."

"Can I see?"

I gave Marnie a tour of my tats—the ones I could show her by rolling up sleeves and pant legs, anyway. I started, as always, with the tiger behind the eight ball. That had been my first piece, seventeen with a fake ID, and distorted and awkward as it was, it was still my favorite.

In return, Marnie gave me a tour of the island. I drove, to get a feel for the car. I was accustomed to being higher up off the ground, in a pig of an SUV that bragged that the environment could kiss my ass, but that I secretly felt guilty for owning. The Town Car's suspension was impeccable. It floated down the narrow roads like we were drifting along on a two-ton cloud. The radio station was tuned to smooth jazz. Definitely an old-man car.

"That house belongs to the Shapiros," Marnie said. "They use it maybe two weeks out of the year."

"So is everybody...gone for the season?" I wasn't really sure why I wanted to hoard my late-night meeting with Anton, tuck it away, and not show it to anyone, even Marnie.

"Harlan Scott's always the last to go. Take a left. We'll swing by his place."

The Scott house was distinctive among the other island properties. Not only did it lack a decorative shingle that read *Scott's*, but it was completely fenced in by a twelve-foot monstrosity that conveyed in no uncertain terms that its single occupant valued his privacy. The *Trespassers WILL be Prosecuted* sign across the gate reinforced this impression.

"Cozy," I said.

"I know it looks bad," said Marnie, "but I've talked to Mr. Scott. He's really not a bad guy, he's just private."

The car idled soundlessly.

"And he's kind of into disaster preparedness."

"What do you mean?"

"Oh, I don't know." We watched a red squirrel dart to the center of the road, tail flicking. It paused, gave us a haughty look, then dashed to the other side and up the tree trunk of a leaning maple. "It wasn't as if he went around passing out pamphlets he'd printed up in his basement or anything, we just got to talking when I ran into him at the grocery store. Sometimes he told me 'the grid' was going to go down. But then sometimes he said a pandemic was long overdue. But really. He's not that weird. Just shy. A good neighbor."

A sprinkling of maple seeds twirled down and tapped on the hood of the car. "So that's it? The Whites are the only ones who stay the winter?"

"And the sculptor, Anton Kopec. I don't know if he'll stay this year. He came pretty early in the spring, so I'm thinking that either the cold doesn't bother him or he's here to get away from the distractions of the city. I'll show you his place. Follow this road to the end, then hang a right."

I followed Marnie's directions, and a house emerged from the woods. It was orange, in a fake-redwood sort of way, and the cutesy mailbox with folk art doves painted on it read *Arnesons*. At least there was no apostrophe. "I thought you said his name was Kopec."

"Right. This is his sister's place. He lives on the property, in one of the outbuildings on the edge of the woods."

I put the car in park, and Marnie opened the passenger door. My heart started racing at the thought of Anton seeing me gawking at his place from the road. And I wondered what he'd look like once I had enough light to actually see him in detail.

Marnie walked across the lawn, and leaves rustled around her feet. "Here," she said, pointing to the mailbox post. "Here's one of his sculptures."

I had to really look hard to pick it out, but when I saw it, finally saw it, a chill raced down my spine. What looked at first like a tangle of dead vines clinging to the mailbox shifted and resolved itself into the withered husk of a creature, as if something had crawled up out of the bowels of hell and then crisped as the sun broke over the horizon and touched it with its rays.

"Whoa," I said.

"Yeah. Tell me about it. They're not all so...what's the word, figurative? But even the abstract ones are still pretty creepy, in a Blair Witch Project kind of way. I don't know how anyone can stand having something like that in their house."

If I had stumbled across art like that, back when I was working twelve-hour days and booking appointments six months out and had more money than I knew what to do with, I would've been all over it, whether I understood it or not. "It's interesting," I said, as noncommittally as I could manage. "He sells them?"

"His sister does. He stays here and does...whatever he does. I make him sound like a slacker, I guess, but that's not it at all. The woods behind his place brush up against the Whites' property." She pointed. "Well, you can see it in the winter, once all the leaves have dropped. Anyway, he's usually up working all night long. Sometimes, if the wind's blowing the right way, you'll pick up the sound of a drill or a staple gun."

I looked at the hellcreature husk and tried to imagine if the wigwam we'd built the night before looked anywhere near as cool.

"You're an artist," Marnie said, "right? Isn't that what you said during the interview? Custom art. I thought you'd meant you did portraits or something."

"Tattoos."

Marnie laughed. "Right. Custom art. That's a good way to describe it. I was going to ask what you thought of this stuff, but I'll bet it's right up your alley." She lowered her voice and leaned toward me, grinning. "Not me. I like a nice landscape. Maybe with a barn on it."

We headed back to the house so that Melita didn't have to hold down the fort by herself. Marnie started lunch, and I sat at the kitchen table with a cup of coffee and read through the description of my duties. I was expected to keep the car detailed and maintained, to be available between ten and seven for errands—earlier and later by prior arrangement. Two nights a week off. "A couple of things, Marnie."

She was grating carrots for a salad. She didn't

look up. "Mm?"

"One, there's hardly fifteen hours of work in this schedule, not unless Mrs. White gets her hair done every single day."

"Will you be busy every hour of every day? No. There's a library half an hour from here. They'll give you a card if you show them your license and a letter from Mrs. stating that you live here."

I'm thinking she knew what the second thing was. I waited for her to address it, but she didn't. She kept on grating.

"I don't see anything about showering people either."

Marnie put down the carrot. "Ray, you've been honest with me. So let's keep things that way. You're not just here to drive the car. You're the muscle." When she spoke, she arranged the carrot gratings into a perfectly symmetrical cone, which brought to mind the Great Pyramid of Giza. "I know it sounds old-fashioned to want a man around the house. That used to be Mr., and when he started forgetting how to get home when they were out on their day trips, Mrs. hired her first driver."

"Melita made it sound like there's been a long line of drivers."

"You're the third. Stanley Marsh worked here for nearly six months, but right around the Fourth of July, he left all of a sudden. Mrs. was beside herself. And then she found Gene."

She spread the grated carrot into a patty and then mounded it into a cone shape again. I kept my mouth shut, though it seemed to me there was more to the story than she was letting on, if it was that difficult for her to find the words to say it.

"Mrs. adored Gene," she said finally.

"But he left all of a sudden too. Did he have a run-in with Mr.?"

Marnie's head snapped up. "Don't say that, Ray. Mr.'s sick, he can't help what he does. Sometimes when I look into his eyes, I think I can see his old personality trapped inside this body that doesn't work right anymore." She flattened the carrots again. "And besides, I know why Gene left. It wasn't anything Mr. did."

I finished my coffee and hoped she wasn't going to make me guess. She put the grater in the dishwasher and started plating up the salad, and finally, she said, "It was me. Gene had this crush on me. I had no idea, not until he said something." She weighed her words even more carefully. "He wasn't my type. It was a really awkward conversation. Beyond awkward."

"Well. You won't have to worry about me putting you on the spot."

She laughed. It sounded a little bit nervous and a lot relieved. "Would you believe that was the first thing that popped into my head when you told me you're gay?"

Chapter Six

Marnie took lunch upstairs to the Whites, while Melita and I ate in the kitchen. "So," I said. "You work here long?"

"Ten years."

Shit. Ten years seemed like forever to me. Ten years ago I'd been backpacking through Europe.

"Anything to...do around here? Off duty?"

She waved her arm toward the kitchen window. "What, you think maybe there's a nightclub on the island, only nobody told you about it?"

I managed not to spit food, but I did shake a little as I stifled down a laugh. "What do you do in your spare time?"

"What spare time? I clean up after everyone, I dust, I vacuum, I scrub the floors, and the next day, it starts all over again."

"But you get two nights a week off," I said, wondering if maybe she was pissed that Marnie had suggested I take Friday and Saturday. "There's got to be something to break up your week."

"I don't need any nights off. I talked to Mrs. White, she pays me overtime instead. I stay here, send the money to my brother in Mexico City."

I ate my pasta, farfalle in a pesto sauce. It was incredible.

"What do I need money for, anyway?" Melita said, after we'd eaten in silence long enough that I thought she was done with the topic. "I live in a good house, I have food. I have my own television, my own phone. My family, they're using the money to send my nieces to school, make sure they get good jobs. We all make out good.

"Besides, it gets too cold up here to go anywhere. Once it starts snowing out, I'd rather stay inside 'til spring comes."

Mrs. White entered the kitchen with an armload of men's shirts draped over her arm, heavy wood hangers dangling. "I was going through Edgar's closet last night, and I realized he hasn't been able to wear these 17-1/2s in such a long time. Would you be interested in them, Raymond? Otherwise, they'll just go to waste."

My typical MO for buying shirts was to go for the XL with the longest sleeves. I glanced down at my cuffs. My ink was covered. "The sleeves might be a little short."

Mrs. White's eyes went to my cuffs too. "Don't worry about that. It's only us here."

I could tell from where I sat that Mr. White's old shirts were crisper, newer, and better made than the ones I'd picked up at the thrift store. It would save me a lot of grief to own more than two dress shirts. I would've thought Mrs. White's offer would rub me the wrong way, make me feel like a charity case—but instead I was touched, maybe from seeing her as vulnerable as she'd been last night. "All right. Thanks."

She draped the shirts over the back of a chair. "I'll leave you to your lunch."

"Good," said Melita, once she'd left. "I thought she had more laundry for me. You need clothes? Gene left most of his stuff behind when he took off. I got 'em in a bag in the laundry room. I don't know how good it would fit, though. He was a couple inches shorter than you, and he had a big belly."

If he was heavy, he might have some XLs that would fit. Melita's warning about the upcoming winter had me spooked. Winter in Traverse City was never fun for anyone but cross-country skiers, and Red Wing Island probably had sharper gusts and higher drifts. "I'll take a look, if you don't mind."

"Don't matter to me. Only one I can think of who'd care is Mrs. White. She treated Gene like he was her own kid. But since she's giving you her husband's clothes, it's probably okay to give you Gene's."

I went through Gene's old stuff and found some long-sleeved T-shirts and sweats that would fit. He had a couple of ties. I took them and his dress socks. His shoes were two sizes too small.

I walked back to my apartment loaded down with clothes, and I wondered if maybe I could stand to adopt Melita's attitude. Sure, I'd had possessions—mostly toys—and I'd lost them. But what did I really need? I had a job, I had a place to stay, and now I even had clothes. Maybe what was daunting me was the isolation.

I'm not a people person, not like Johnny, who'd had so many friends he couldn't begin to count them all. (Though you have to wonder how many of those were friends and how many were people he got high with.) I was no social butterfly, but I wasn't a loner either. Tattoo art isn't solitary. Once you've inked everything you can reach on your own body, you've got to start working on other people.

Here, I had only the Whites, Melita, and Marnie for company.

And Anton. Assuming he'd want to see more of me, which seemed premature. And exciting.

I was so wrapped up in mentally undressing Anton, scoping out that sexy mouth of his with my tongue, running my fingers down his long, lean body, under the waistband of his jeans, that I barely swerved in time.

Gore splattered the walkway and the threshold of the door to my front stairs, startlingly red. I staggered into the grass, felt something soft and wet give way under the sole of my shoe.

It didn't stink of fish this time. No feathers clinging to the guts. Instead, fur stuck out here and there in little tufts. I recalled the squirrel who'd watched Marnie giving me the tour of the island. I'm sure it couldn't possibly have been the very same squirrel—or what was left of him— here. But I couldn't help but think of it that way.

"Foxes," Mrs. White said. She sat in the backseat of the Town Car, speaking to the back of my head. I had my eyes on the narrow, winding road, and half my brain wondering if she saw through my hair to the Celtic knot at the base of my skull. "Mr. Scott—he's very familiar with wildlife—tells me that he has never seen, nor heard, coyotes on the island. But there are foxes."

"Scott. He's the, um...." Crackpot survivalist. How had Marnie put it? "...the guy who's into disaster preparedness."

"Yes, Harlan Scott. He's kept a summer home on the island for almost twenty years now. He usually stays through October, so I'm surprised he's gone already. Although, he really isn't the sort to stop over and say goodbye. He tends to keep to himself."

I guided the car over the bridge, which felt

sturdy enough, but sounded hollow beneath the tires. It was a relief to hit the two-lane that led to town.

"Did you sleep well last night?" she asked me.

"Fine, I guess. Strange bed and all. And it sounds different on the island than it does in the city." And maybe I'd been listening to see if I might hear Anton romping through the woods again. And maybe I wondered if he was busy TP-ing my front door with entrails in some bizarre, postmodern initiation ritual.

"Edgar used to say that, and also that the air was different on the island too. He felt like he slept more deeply here than he ever did in the city."

"So you didn't always live here year-round."

"No, not until Edgar retired. We always looked forward to coming and hated leaving, until finally we decided to sell our condo and stay."

Mrs. White had me escort her to all the pit stops, which was fine by me. I'd rather walk around than just sit there in the car and stare at the windshield. We stopped for a late lunch at a trendy coffee shop with sandwiches that looked a lot better than they tasted.

"I'm spoiled by Marnie's cooking," Mrs. White told me. "She should really be working in a fancy hotel. But she says she wouldn't care for the hours."

I was raising my chicken club for another bite when the door opened and three twentysomethings wandered in, all jeans and leather and crayon-bright hair.

And Johnny. Shit.

It was a small town, and I was bound to see him sooner or later...but I'd really been hoping it would be later. He'd colored his hair cherry red and sprayed it up into a short fin, but even though I'd never seen him as a redhead, the tat on his neck, a thorny vine, was hard to miss. I'd designed that piece myself.

It was almost one thirty. He'd probably just rolled out of bed. Probably someone else's bed. Probably the bed that belonged to the pink-haired girl in the leopard-skin coat, and her boyfriend with a complexion like skimmed milk. I turned away from them and studied the stand-up display on the table that encouraged us to make dinner special by taking home a whole pie: apple, cherry, or pecan.

I looked at that pie ad so hard I'm surprised I didn't burn a hole through it. The pink-haired girl laughed, and the violent hiss of the espresso machine muted the sound. It occurred to me that I didn't know which overpriced coffee drink Johnny would have ordered. Because I'd seldom just hung out with him; I was too busy working.

The time it took to make three drinks was excruciating. Thank God they took their mocha-whipped-latte-whatevers and hit the road. If they'd opted to stay, no amount of twisting and turning would've kept Johnny from spotting me.

"You didn't want your friends to see you with an old lady," Mrs. White said.

"What?"

She smiled, a bit sadly. "You were trying very hard not to be seen."

"Oh." I hadn't realized it'd been that obvious. "Not because of you. It was...." What *was* my problem, anyway? Was it that I couldn't stand for Johnny to see me in a tie? Fuck that. He thought it was "cool" to drift from bed to bed because he was too lazy to earn his keep, so I'd be damned if I let him look down on me for earning a living. No, it was more that I just couldn't stand the sight of him. "They weren't friends of mine. Just... someone I used to know."

We finished our lunch and hit a couple more stores; then Mrs. White stopped to visit with a friend before we headed back. I read the Town Car's owner's manual from front to back—twice—by the time she was done. "I hear there's a library in town," I said. Because I hoped that maybe she would add it to her list of stops.

"It's just up the road."

I waited for her to suggest we stop. She didn't. "This road?" I prompted.

"Over there. By the pizzeria."

"Did you...need any books?"

"They're closed on Thursdays. Tax cuts, you know. Not enough circulation to hire another staff member."

I sighed.

"You're welcome to borrow any of my books you'd like."

"I don't know that we'd have the same taste in reading material."

I glanced in the rearview and saw Mrs. White smile. "You're probably right. I don't see you as the Jane Austen type. You should pay a visit to Mr. Kopec, in the redwood house on the other side of the woods. You'll probably have more in common with him. He's right around your age, and he's into all those 'artistic' sorts of things."

I assumed she meant my ink. Probably. "You've seen his artwork?"

"I have. Very different. His sister's friend represents him. She has a gallery in Detroit. His work sells better in a big city than it would around here."

"He makes a living at it?" I was surprised; I'd had the impression that he'd be destitute without his sister.

"He does rather well, so I've heard."

"Then how come he lives in his sister's guesthouse?"

"You'll have to ask Mr. Kopec. He's never mentioned it to me."

I'd been fishing for a trip to the library and found myself with an airtight excuse to get another look at Anton instead. After dinner, I

mentioned Mrs. White's book-borrowing sugges-
tion to Marnie. It wasn't my night off, but since
both Marnie and Melita were home, and since
Mrs. White had actually suggested it, I suspected
I could get away with abandoning my post.

"Wait a minute," Marnie said. "Before you go."
She went into the utility room off the kitchen,
and I heard the sound of drawers opening and
closing. She came back with a rubber mallet. "I
borrowed it from him a couple of months ago.
Bring this with you—that way, if he's in a mood,
you can just say you were returning it for me, and
you can take off again."

"A mood."

"You know." Her hand fluttered, as if it would
help her locate the right word. Evidently, it failed.
"A mood."

Whatever. "You got a flashlight too? Someone
keeps leaving presents on my doorstep."

"I've been thinking about that. Someone
must've brought a cat with them this summer
and left it behind. Probably the Shapiros—too
busy checking their stock portfolios to notice
that Fluffy's missing. If you want, I can pick up
some cat food when I get groceries tomorrow."

"For what?"

"Put a bowl of food and a bowl of water outside
your door. If it likes you enough to leave you
presents, maybe you can tame it."

"You think I need a cat."

"Why not? I don't think Mrs. would mind, especially if it was an outdoor cat that just kind of
eased its way in. This island's a lonely place when
roads drift over and you're waiting for the snow-
plows to dig you out."

There was one creature on the island I was
hoping could ease that loneliness, but he wasn't
of the feline variety.

I wished I had something to put in my hair to
make it look less Wall Street. I went through the
medicine cabinet to see if Gene had left anything
behind, but given that no one had made him
out to be the type of guy to spike his hair up, I
wasn't surprised to find nothing but dental floss
and cheap aftershave.

I changed into my real clothes—jeans, T-shirt,
biker boots, and leather jacket—and headed
through the woods to see a man about some
books. The sun was down by the time I'd dressed.
I took the flashlight and the mallet and tried to
figure out where, exactly, I'd built wigwams by
the light of the full moon two nights before. It
took me nearly half an hour. I'd tripped over
several tree roots and nearly broke my ankle
in a gopher hole, but I found the stick pyramid.
And three others just like it that had sprung up
around it.

The original pyramid had looked kind of artsy
in the moonlight.

The four of them together in the flashlight

beam looked a little creepy.

I circled around the pyramids and inched through the trees until I saw a pair of windows glowing yellow in the thick, cicada-droning darkness. I tripped over another tree root, staggered, then did my best to stay upright as I made my way toward Anton's house.

It was a tiny thing, maybe twenty by twenty, with five steps leading up to a narrow porch with a dilapidated rocking chair on it, and a wind chime made of dozens of small, fragile white bones. I wondered if he'd shot any photos of the time he'd redecorated his sister's house. I was guessing he and I had similar taste.

Music seeped through the front door, mostly bass, a thudding beat—nothing I recognized right off the bat, but maybe it wasn't something that was meant to be sung along with. Maybe it was more of a trance inducement. I pressed my fingertips to the frame of his storm door and felt a faint vibration. It would be loud inside, but the house was very well insulated. I looked for a doorbell. There was none. So I opened the storm door and knocked on the leaded glass pane of the front door. Hard.

The music cut. The door opened, and there he was—Anton, framed like a vision in bright yellow light. I'd been worried that maybe the light of the full moon had played tricks on me, that maybe once I got a really good look at him, the spell would be broken and I'd see that he was just some guy. A guy with black hair down to his shoulders and finger bones dangling from his porch, but just a guy, nonetheless.

I'd been wrong. Up close and well lit, Anton was a wet dream.

He looked me over and smiled, and that hairline gap between his front teeth was startlingly hot. "Ray of Moonlight, fellow insomniac and pyramid craftsman. I've been wondering if I'd really met you the other night or if I'd just invented you to amuse myself. But here you are." He glanced down at the flashlight and mallet. "And you brought toys."

I stepped inside. He backed up far enough to let me get in the door and no farther. "I hear you're a big-time gallery artist."

"So they say. I have no empirical proof. Diane's worried I might be myself in front of the art scene and blow my reputation, so she's billed me as some kind of socially retarded recluse so she can handle all the deals without me."

"Maybe that's for the best. Dealers would try to steer you toward making things they can sell. Maybe it's easier to be true to your art when you don't have to deal with any of that shit."

He tilted his head back and stared at my lips with sultry-lidded eyes. "Spoken like a true artist."

"You could say that."

"I just did."

"I wasn't always a driver, you know. My license is so new it squeaks when I put it in my wallet."

Anton dropped his gaze to my jacket, my chest, then raked it back up to my eyes again. Either he practiced seductive looks in the mirror, or it just came naturally to him. And he didn't strike me as the type of guy who was able to slap on a false front—if he would even bother to.

"You can tell me what you were before, or not. I like to think we reinvent ourselves each and every day. Even our cells shed and regenerate. We're literally not the same person we were seven years ago."

"That might explain why I do such stupid things," I said. And the way Anton stood right up in my space, the way neither one of us backed off, I suspected I was on the verge of adding one more act of dubious intelligence to my collection. "I was an artist."

"Was? I don't think the artistic temperament is something you can misplace. Once it finds you, you're stuck with it." Anton straightened the lapel of my jacket. Blood surged downward. He hadn't even touched me yet, not any more than my jacket, but my body was giving me the green light already.

"The artistic temperament's a bunch of bullshit. Something trust-fund kids at art school use as an excuse to leech off other people." Or more accurately, a label used by people like Johnny to make a sucker out of people like me. "I had my own business."

"Better you than me. I always thought the more I owned, the more it tied me down. One day I'll probably hike out into the middle of nowhere and live off the land. But those other idiots you're talking about, the self-styled *artistes*? I've got less use for 'em than you do. So even though I like to bitch about it, I'm sure I'm not missing much by letting Diane handle the galleries."

Anton stared me in the eye while he talked, and never broke eye contact. I can stare anybody down, but his unflinching attention had me unsettled. "I didn't come here to psychoanalyze myself," I said. "I'm just returning a hammer."

My lapels were lying flat, but Anton smoothed them again while he watched for my reaction. If I even had one, it was subtle. I stood there, close, and I stared back at him while his hands moved up my chest and over my shoulders. He shifted, and our thighs brushed. I stood my ground. Then he grabbed my head two-handed, cupped my jaw, and pulled himself even closer, excruciatingly close, into an almost-kiss I was just on the verge of feeling. I closed my eyes and breathed. He smelled male. And different from Johnny, which was good.

I slid off my leather jacket, let it drop to the floor with the flashlight and mallet inside the sleeves. I eased my body against his, felt his breath on my lips. His grip on my jaw tightened. He eased forward too, until gradually, finally, his mouth pressed against mine. That first kiss was slow and deliberate. It lingered, as if we both needed to get our bearings. Anton pulled away first, but only to speak. He pressed his forehead to mine. "Did my sister hire you to keep me from going blind?"

I mouthed the word *blind* against his lips.

"Excessive masturbating." He traced my cheekbones with his thumbs and stared into my eyes.

"Nope. Your sister's got zero to do with me."

Anton's eyes narrowed. He cocked his head. "That's probably the hottest thing I've ever heard. Which shows you how pathetic my life is lately."

He leaned in for another kiss, and this time, he eased his tongue into my mouth. I put my hands on his hips. He felt slimmer than Johnny. Taller too, almost as tall as me. And I told myself to quit comparing, but how could I stop? That's just the way it is, when you've been with someone for a couple of years and you're still smarting where they've stung you.

Anton slid one hand around the back of my neck and wove his fingers through my hair. His other hand dropped, made its way underneath my T-shirt. His breath hissed in, cool over my lips. "It's been so long since I touched someone," he said, "it feels like it happened in another life."

Another life? That described the way I'd been feeling lately so well that it made the hair on my forearms prickle.

I ran my hands up and down Anton's sides. He had one of those wiry builds that he either nurtured by jogging and biking, or by fretting away his calories with caffeine and nicotine. Or maybe he was one of those naturally thin people who can live on Yoo-hoo and doughnuts and never gain a pound.

Anton took hold of my T-shirt and pulled it over my head. It was cool in his tiny guesthouse, but the tightly coiled anticipation in my gut made considerations like "hot" and "cold" seem negligible.

"Oh," was all he said, when he saw my ink. Just a syllable. And I'd been waiting for recognition to kick in, for him to tell me that inking tats made me an artist as much as picking a box in the football pool made someone an athlete, but from the sound of his voice—soft and filled with wonder—I could tell he saw what I saw in it. Even if he did sell stuff at some shi-shi gallery. Or his sister did.

He touched my cloud dragon, my densest, most colorful piece, which covered me from ribs to shoulder to elbow on my left side. He nodded, very grave. "This is good."

"Thanks."

He traced a lightning bolt that wrapped my

ribs, and a shiver rippled through my body. "All of it's yours?"

"Not all. Most of the newer pieces. It's slow going, inking yourself." I hadn't been prepared for the experience of meeting people who didn't know me as Ray from Body Art Studio...the now-defunct Body Art Studio. It made my tats feel exotic. Maybe taboo.

The way it'd felt when I got that tiger and eight ball. Several lifetimes ago.

Anton dragged his fingertip along the clouds, over to my right side, where a gargoyle crouched. "No piercings? I'm surprised."

"I hate needles." The sight of them poking through to the opposite side of whatever's being pierced, anyway.

He nodded, lifted up my arm to get a good look at the gargoyle's expression. I'd had the gargoyle's face done by my favorite apprentice, a skinny girl named Alice with more holes in her than I could count. She'd had a good, steady hand.

I held still while Anton moved around me, stroking my body as he read my skin. I stared at the wall straight ahead. Something that looked like a cross between a dried apple-head doll, a pair of mummified testicles, and a souvenir from a fateful trip down the Amazon hung over a filthy microwave splattered with tomato sauce and grease.

It was repulsive, whatever it was—the sculpture, not the microwave. Yet I couldn't stop looking. And I supposed, again, that if I was flush with cash, I'd buy it in a second.

Anton sidled around me in a crouch, passed the cloud dragon, and hitched his fingers into my belt buckle. They were long fingers, stained with dirt or pigment. "Show me the rest." He tugged at my waistband.

"It's your turn to take something off," I said.

"My tribal markings are nowhere near as colorful." He crossed his arms, grabbed the tattered hem of his gray, long-sleeved thermal top, and pulled the shirt over his head.

His body was already winter pale, like someone who can't be bothered with the sun. The dusting of hair on his chest looked stark against his white skin, and it occurred to me that he didn't dye his hair, which was unheard of in my most recent social circles.

He dropped his thermal shirt and pointed to a crescent-shaped scar alongside his stomach. "Age nine. Ruptured appendix." He flipped his arm over and showed me the underside of his wrist. A thick ridge of white scar tissue crossed his forearm, an inch below the base of his palm. "Age eighteen. Suicide attempt. Unsuccessful, obviously." He smirked. "Don't worry, I've been out of that phase for years."

He held out his right arm. "Ditto." The scar on

that wrist was thinner, less pronounced. I guessed that he was right-handed, unable to slice himself as decisively with his left hand. Either that, or he'd already cut his left wrist, and the amount of blood that must have been spreading had given him second thoughts.

I glanced at the apple-head testicle thing. Maybe not.

Anton flipped his arm over and pointed to a couple of small puncture mark scars. "Neighbor's Chihuahua. Age eleven. Me, not the dog. I don't know exactly how old the dog was. Maybe he was eleven too."

I wrapped my fingers around his scarred forearm and pulled him against me, skin to skin. Our mouths met. They fit together more readily than they had the first time. That was all it took, I supposed, to get used to somebody. A single kiss. It didn't seem like nearly enough of a prerequisite. But I was glad, and ready to forget whatever traces of Johnny were still left on me, wipe the slate clean for someone new.

Anton rubbed his whole body against mine. His hands raked me, anywhere he could touch, over my ribs, down my back. A quick squeeze of my ass, then greedy between my legs, cupping me, feeling me.

My breath caught. Anton covered my mouth with a deep, bold kiss. My cock stiffened beneath his roaming hands.

I turned my mouth away from his. "I don't have any condoms," I said. Because I didn't have much of anything. Not anymore.

"Good. Then we won't have to fight about who gets to use up his rubbers before they expire." He took me by the waistband of my jeans and towed me into the bathroom. It was incredibly small, just enough to fit a toilet, shower stall, and sink, cramped enough that he probably stepped out into his studio so he could get dressed without banging his elbows on the towel bar. He flipped the toilet seat shut, unbuttoned my jeans, pulled them down around my knees, and gave me a shove. I sat down hard.

He opened a medicine cabinet above my head, and cotton swabs and safety razors rained down on me. "One look at you and I'm dying to suck some minty-good latex."

He dropped a green foil strip into my lap. Mint. Then he knelt down between my knees and looked up at me impatiently. I tore off a condom, checked the date. Still a few months left. I opened the foil, rolled it on. Good thing I'd been cultivating a steady hand for twenty years; otherwise, he would've seen me shaking.

Not that I was nervous. Well, actually, I was. But it felt more like shock. Everything was too new. This room, this man. This island. Me. Seven years to shed my cells and become a new person? Hell, I was a different guy than I'd been seven months ago. I looked down at my tiger and eight ball to reassure myself that I was still me—because lately, when I'd glanced down and seen the buttoned cuff of a white oxford dress shirt instead of the studded bracelet and ink-smeared latex glove, I'd felt like a ghost who was too stubborn to move into the light and had ended up possessing some Mr. Average America who'd been too oblivious to notice the hijacking of his own body.

Anton grabbed the base of my cock and exerted enough pressure to make things interesting. My body responded by flooding my groin. I went from hard to super hard. He bent his head to me and planted a long, wet lick across my balls, and I shuddered from my scalp to the soles of my feet.

I buried my hands in his hair, felt it glide like silk through my fingers, unhampered by spray or gel or paste or wax or whatever the new, hip product might be. Me, not me...I stopped dwelling on it, swept away by the touch of his hair, the heat of his mouth.

Anton seemed as hungry for me as I felt for him. He swallowed me deep and grunted his satisfaction as my cockhead bumped his throat. All the while, his hands roved over my hips and thighs as if they could never manage to touch enough of my skin.

I moaned out loud. I'm not a screamer, but the feel of his mouth closing over me was so incredible, so right, it dredged the noise up from somewhere inside me I hadn't even realized was there.

Anton made a noise in return. An encouragement. And he started stroking my balls in time with his sucking, until finally I couldn't watch anymore, and I tilted my head back and focused on the feeling. The heat. The pressure. The trail of saliva that slipped down past the ring of his finger and thumb, the base of the condom, and rolled, startlingly wet, down my nuts while he stroked them.

I saw the brink coming already—fast, but hell, it'd been so long since I'd been with anyone it was hardly surprising. The strangeness of it all, the unfamiliarity of everything, including myself, clicked into place and dragged me toward the edge.

Anton must have sensed it in the clench of my thighs. He backed off.

He kept his finger and thumb locked around the base of the condom, and he pulled off with a slurp so loud it rang against the tiles. I opened my eyes, just a crack, as he threw his long hair back and gave me a dazzlingly naughty smile.

I probably looked stunned. I sure felt that way.

He stood and ran a hand over the bulge in his jeans, then caught one of my hands and pressed it against him so I could feel his stiff cock through the denim. "Let's go to bed."

I fished the strips of condoms off the floor

where they lay among the scattered cotton swabs, a few crumpled tissues, and an empty prescription bottle. Anton grabbed me by the arm and dragged me out into the studio. The farthest corner was hidden by a folding screen that might have been kitschy once, but had been painted, textured, sanded, and repainted so many times, and in the loose, decayed way that Anton handled every medium he touched, that it looked like something that'd been scavenged from an abandoned movie set that was buried by an earthquake.

The screen hid a twin bed with mismatched sheets and pillows, unmade. Nothing else. I shuffled behind Anton with my jeans around my ankles. He spun me and pushed me back onto the bed.

"Take off your pants," I said. "And leave the light on."

"Lights-out never crossed my mind. There's too much of you I haven't seen yet."

We both stripped off our jeans while we kept our eyes glued to each other. Anton's inkless body looked like a blank canvas, no markings other than his battle scars. I couldn't remember the last time I'd been with someone who didn't have any tats—even if it was only an unfortunate cartoon character they'd chosen from a wall of flash on a teenage impulse.

Strangely enough, I didn't itch to fill that

canvas with whorls and spikes and gradations of color. I just wanted to enjoy it for what it was, like a blanket of fresh snow that makes the world white and clean, if only for a few hours, before the pollution settles and turns everything a uniform shade of gray.

"You're tattooing me with your eyes," Anton said.

I pried off my boots and sank back onto my elbows. "No. Just the opposite."

"Flaying me?"

"You've got one fucked-up sense of humor."

"I try." He stepped between my feet, leading with his hips in that odd sashay of his—leading with his cock, I realized, now that it was pointing at me, hard and thick, red. He ran his fingertips along the barbed wire piece that snaked down my leg. "It balances the dragon."

Anton straddled my leg and stroked his hard cock. I stared at the fleshy head, appearing and disappearing within the loose grasp of his pigment-stained fingers. He crouched and touched his cockhead to my barbed wire tattoo where it bisected my thigh. He let out a shuddery breath when his bare skin glided over mine, and I realized that I hadn't been breathing either.

His eyes roamed my body—or maybe just my ink—while he stroked himself and petted my thigh with the tip of his cock. I watched him looking at me, and I fixed the line of his cheekbone and jaw, the pattern where his dark stubble came in, the tilt of his head and the shadows his long eyelashes cast.

Anton let go of his cock and brushed his fingertips over my balls. "How do you want to do this?"

"Every way we can."

He caught his lower lip in his teeth, flashing that sexy gap, and twitched his eyebrows. "Good answer."

He rolled on a condom and lay on top of me. More kisses, starting slow, then building in depth, intensity. He ground into me, and my cock found the hollow inside his hip bone. I stroked myself on him while his tongue learned my mouth and left me breathless.

He broke the kiss. Our hips had locked into a rhythm, rubbing our cocks against each other's bodies sure and hard, so good I might come just from rocking against him and kissing his hypnotic mouth.

But Anton reached under the bed, groped for a moment, and came up with a plastic bottle of lube. He flipped the cap up with his teeth and squirted some into his palm as he eased up into a kneeling position.

"Try this on for size," he said. He pulled the mint condom off and grabbed me hard, stroked my cock with his slippery hand.

My back arched up, and I gave a guttural moan.

"Very nice, Ray of Moonlight. Can I bury myself

in your colorful ass while I do my best to make you make that noise again?"

I wasn't exactly thinking in words anymore. I nodded.

Anton slicked his condom with lube, then hooked his forearms behind my legs and folded my knees toward my chest. "I'm dying to see the story unfold on your back," he said, "but right now, I'd rather watch your face when you come."

My cock twitched. Johnny had never said anything like that...in fact, he hadn't been able to rub two words together in bed. Tired, high, going through the motions, who knows? I was usually the one on top too—at first because I was more experienced, and eventually, because Johnny realized he preferred to lie there looking pretty, rather than expending any actual effort.

"Second thoughts?" Anton said.

I hadn't realized he could see it in my eyes when I was revisiting Johnny. I shook my head.

"Good."

His cock prodded my hole, big—damn it, I might as well be a virgin again. "Go slow," I said. My voice was sandpapery.

"Yeah, let's make it last," he said. He stopped pushing and swirled lube over my ass with his cockhead. The room was filled with the sound of our breathing and the crinkle of the reservoir tip.

He swiped my ass and retreated, swiped and retreated, until finally I was ready to beg. "Not that slow," I said.

Anton treated me to a very naughty smile. "Just making sure." He lined himself up and pushed, and I let my breath out, did my best to relax. Both of us moaned, him, me, and I rode on the high of my ass so full of cock that it was painful—a delicious sort of pain that would make my balls tingle, days later, from the mere thought of him sinking it in.

Anton turned his head and dragged his tongue over the inside of my knee, then raked my skin with his teeth while he hugged my thigh to his chest. "How's that?" he said. It was a whisper.

"Feels good."

His breath was hot and moist on the crook of my knee as he pushed in deep. My cock was slick with lube. I stroked it gently while the painful pleasure intensified, and every nerve ending in my body seemed to coalesce in my groin. Anton pulled out and pushed in again, slow, but deep. Again, and again.

"I wanna pound you so bad," he said.

My cock throbbed. I was ready. "Do it."

Anton let his body weight drop onto my thighs, and my knees pressed toward my shoulders. My breath whooshed out, and I had a hard time catching it. His face hovered over mine, black hair hanging down, tickling my cheeks, forming a wall that narrowed my world to nothing but his dark eyes.

His thrusts picked up speed, but he never pulled out more than partway, kept his cock half buried. He moved faster. His balls slapped against my ass, softly at first, then louder. Pretty soon he was fucking me hard.

I was so tangled up in my knees and my inability to draw even one single deep breath that my orgasm sideswiped me, and I made a strange, strangled sound, eyes wide open, staring up into Anton's eager face.

He grabbed my shoulders as I shot, and pulled us together so tightly it was as if he was trying to merge us. The breathlessness, the sweet-edged pain—it uncoiled deep in my gut, and I came so hard, it was as if the word *orgasm* could hardly describe the sensation.

And then I realized that Anton was still and just watching me, staring down at my face. My eyes were still open, but it might have been a few seconds since I'd actually seen anything.

"That was beautiful," he whispered.

Chapter Seven

It was a wonder I emerged from the woods any-where near the Whites' property. My knees were so rubbery that they couldn't quite carry me in a straight line, and my brain wasn't paying any attention where I was headed either.

Anton had tried to convince me to stay. He'd very nearly succeeded. But I'd agreed to two nights off each week, and tonight wasn't one of them. I'd gone to Anton's to return a mallet and borrow a book. It was suspicious enough that it'd taken me two hours to do so.

Especially since I'd forgotten to ask him for a book.

I pushed through the undergrowth and found myself at the front of the house, where a gazebo covered in withering vines stood, drifted with leaves.

I staggered past the gazebo toward the house, leaves rustling all around me. I glanced over my shoulder at the structure and staggered back. A silhouette I'd taken for a tree moved in a very untreelike way, and it resolved itself into the shape of a man.

Three steps back, I finally found the button of the flashlight, even though it was right under my thumb the whole time. I swung the beam at the phantom in the gazebo, and the figure turned.

Mr. White.

My relief was so palpable I felt giddy. "Mr. White? What're you doing?" I said, before it occurred to me that he couldn't answer.

And yet, he did. His eyes went wide, and he shielded them from the flashlight beam with an outstretched palm. "Who are you?"

I swung the light from his eyes and aimed it at myself. "It's Ray. The driver." Mr. White looked puzzled. I didn't think he remembered meeting me, and given the circumstances, that was probably for the best. "I'm new."

"Where's Stanley?" he said.

I was pretty sure the previous driver's name was Gene. Stanley must've been the first driver then. "He left," I said, and I decided it was best to keep the explanation simple. "I don't really know the whole story, just that I'm his replacement."

Mr. White nodded and squinted at me. I kept the flashlight on my face and took a few steps forward so he could have a look at me. I'm not sure what I expected. That he'd mix me up with this Stanley guy or lapse into confused silence, or maybe that he'd mingle past and present and take me for some long-dead brother of his, or worse, his father. But instead he surprised me. He laughed. "They must've found him playing with the safe. He did that every time he thought no one was looking. Especially me."

He looked up at the moon, which was waning now, but just shy of full. "It's cold out here. Walk me back to the house, if you don't mind.... What did you say your name was?"

"Ray."

"Shine that thing on the ground, Mr. Ray. I don't want to fall and break my neck."

I offered Mr. White my arm, and he took it. We walked together, arm in arm like a couple of old friends, up the porch stairs to the front door. I opened the door. Mrs. White was on her way down the staircase in a robe with her hair wrapped in a towel. "Edgar? Raymond, I almost didn't recognize you." She looked from Mr. White, to me, and back to him again. "Were you outside?"

"I was just checking on the gazebo. I thought I heard something."

"It's pitch dark out there. You could have hurt yourself."

Maybe I'd thought the same thing, but Mrs. White wasn't going to score any points if she impugned her husband's manliness. "We're all in one piece," I told her. "I had a flashlight on me." I kept my tone easy and turned to Mr. White. "You ready to go back upstairs now?"

He considered. "All right. Yes. I'd like to sit down."

"Why don't I walk with you? I was going that way anyway." And even though there couldn't have possibly been anything I needed upstairs— and in fact, I'd never seen more than the route between the bathroom and the bedroom—Mr. White seemed to understand that if I wanted to spin out a little fantasy where we were just a couple of regular guys, it wasn't because I was mocking him. He might forget who I was by morning, and I might have to get into the shower with him again, but for right now, at least, that's what we were. A couple of guys.

I got Mr. White settled in a well-used wingback chair in his bedroom, and turned to go downstairs. Mrs. White approached me in the hall. "He gets restless sometimes and wanders. It's impossible to watch him twenty-four hours a day."

"Maybe you should hire a nurse. There are male nurses, you know."

"Raymond." She slipped her hand through my arm. It rested against the sleeve of my leather jacket, parchment skin and a diamond band that was worth easily as much as the Town Car. "Come with me."

We went down the back stairs together, past Melita's room where a laugh track from some inane comedy swelled through the closed door, and into the kitchen. Mrs. White filled the teapot and put it on the stove. "I promised Edgar, no nurses. So until he can't possibly know the difference, I will keep that promise."

"But you could always say it's just a new maid."

She took two mugs down from the cupboard, added tea bags, and set one in front of me without asking whether I wanted it or not. "This spring, maybe I'll look into it. But, Raymond, you see how it is. He has these moments where he's his old self again, and I couldn't stand to have him realize that I'd done something he specifically asked me not to do."

I nodded and looked at the bright logo on the tea bag tag. It had a little saying on the back. *A wise man's actions speak for themselves.*

The teakettle whistled, and Mrs. White filled both our mugs. "I'm going to go up and be with Edgar until he falls asleep. He seems calmer after he's been with you."

I shrugged and dunked my tea bag.

"Thank you, Raymond."

I couldn't quite meet her eye for some reason. "S'okay," I said.

I steeped my tea, hunted for sugar unsuccessfully, then drank it down black. Marnie had been right—I wished I had met Edgar before the Alzheimer's took him. He seemed like an okay guy.

All the money anyone could ever want, and still his life was shit. I'd thought money, or the lack of it, was to blame for all my problems, so I found the idea that money can't solve every problem hard to wrap my head around.

"I wondered why the light was on."

Marnie. I flinched and wondered how many millions of miles away I'd been when she came in. "Just...thinking."

"Mrs. said you found Mr. outside. I won't lie, it scares the heck out of me that just enough of him comes to the surface to get him in trouble." She pulled a chair out, sat down, and crossed her legs. She had on a pair of backless slippers, and she jiggled one loosely on her foot. "And that's what you were wearing when you caught him?"

I looked down at my leather jackct. "What?"

"You were at Anton's this whole time? And you got dressed up to go there?"

"I'm not 'dressed up.'"

"You think he's gay, don't you?"

I tried to get a read on where Marnie was going with the whole line of questioning, but all I got from her tone of voice was "intense." "Yeah," I told her, "I do. Any particular reason you're busting my balls over it?"

She slumped against the back of the chair. "Just be careful."

"Can you be a little more specific?"

Marnie's leg jiggled harder. The slipper flapped

against the sole of her foot. "Don't expect too much. Like I said, he's moody."

"Moody."

"He was probably being all charming with you—that makes sense, if he's 'up,' and he's into guys, like you say. But he stays awake for days at a time, making all that creepy stuff, and then his temper...."

"Marnie," I said. She stopped talking and looked me in the eye. "I'm a big boy."

She sighed. "Yeah, I know. But you haven't seen him freak out over something. Don't say I didn't warn you."

"Consider me warned."

She got up and put my mug in the dishwasher. "Don't forget to turn the lights off when you're done in here."

"I won't."

Silence, then, except the flap of her slippers on the tile. She stopped in the doorway. "Is your hair wet?"

I touched the back of my head, which confirmed it. And I still smelled like his soap, his shampoo.

"You slept with him already? My God."

I stood and walked toward her and didn't hesitate to tower over her as I reached past her shoulder and turned off the light. "I'm an adult, remember? Good night, Marnie."

Marnie seemed cooler to me after that. Nothing overt, just a harder set to her mouth, more abruptness when we talked. I turned over the events of that first night with Anton in my head. I'd walked through the woods, spent a couple of hours, and come home. What went on while I was there? No one else's business.

So, what was she all ticked off about?

She'd told me her relationship with Gene had gone sour, not only to the point of him quitting, but him quitting without a word to anyone and leaving all his stuff and his last paycheck behind. Maybe I'd just read her wrong initially and she was actually the source of all the drama. Lord knows I'd known enough head cases who seemed perfectly normal at first.

The next morning, the gardening crew came from town in an extended-cab pickup and set to work on getting all the leaves corralled into a burnable pile. I washed and waxed the Town Car while Melita and the lawn crew supervisor chewed the fat in Spanish, which I speak maybe five words of, and which makes even the most mundane conversations sound fast paced and gripping to my ears.

The air was filled with the sound of leaf blowers,

and the Whites' estate buzzed with activity. And when it was time to come in for lunch, I realized that I hadn't thought about Body Art Studio all day. Not once.

Melita quit lunch early to go outside and gossip with the supervisor some more, which left Marnie and me at the table. "It's Friday," she said.

I nodded and waited for her to go somewhere with that.

"You get six to ten off. Tomorrow night too. Stanley used to go into town a lot, stay over. He had some friends there."

I kept on nodding, eating.

"I imagine you'll stay at Anton's."

"I imagine I will, if he seems agreeable to that."

We were both nodding by that time. It was catchy. Difficult to stop.

"Your apartment is your apartment. You can have visitors up there."

"What are you saying?"

"Nothing. I just thought I'd tell you. You don't have to sneak around."

"Who's sneaking?"

"The main thing is that you're here if we need you. Just in case."

In case an accident went beyond something that could be washed down the drain. "I got it."

Marnie stood up and rifled through a drawer. "Cell phone coverage is spotty here—not that you've ever mentioned owning a cell phone—but two-way radios work great. The range covers the whole island." She pulled something that looked like a cell phone with a black rubber antenna out of the drawer and put it on the table. "Gene had one, but he took it with him when he left. This was Mr.'s. He doesn't know how to use it anymore, so you might as well keep it on you. That way, after work, you can go where you want, and nobody's got to worry. Just keep it turned on and tuned to channel twelve."

I wasn't sure if the phone represented freedom or just the opposite. I figured if the walkie-talkie got intrusive, I'd cross that bridge when I came to it. "Okay."

Since I wasn't being called upon to drive Mrs. White anywhere, and the car was spotless, I went outside to watch the landscapers work. While I was eating lunch they'd piled the leaves at the far corner of the property and set them on fire. Two of the workers were unloading a big piece of heavy equipment from the back of the truck, while the third guy wandered in and out of the trees, blowing out the last few leaves, and the supervisor kept gossiping with Melita.

The machine, some kind of digger, had a gas motor that was loud enough to let you know it meant business. I leaned beside the garage with my arms crossed and watched the landscapers do their thing. And I realized I hadn't lived anywhere with a lawn since I was a kid.

Lunch had ended with prosciutto melon rolls fastened by toothpicks, and I'd kept one of the toothpicks to give my hands something to do. I've never smoked—unhygienic when you're tattooing, if you ask me—but I was beginning to see the appeal of keeping my hands busy.

I'd gotten one end of the round toothpick chewed flat by the time Anton slinked around the side of the garage, head-to-toe black, long coat, wild hair, and five days of stubble. "I had absolutely no idea that a tie and a button-down would do it for me," he murmured. "You look like a thug playing dress-up."

Bullshit. Though I'll admit I got a charge out of the idea that Anton didn't find me laughable in the work getup. "What're you up to today?"

"Seeing what's so frickin' loud." He stood beside me and mirrored my pose, arms crossed. "That's one massive rototiller."

The name of the bucking, droning, loud-as-hell machine gave me no indication of what it was actually supposed to be doing, but I figured the landscapers were the experts.

"It's Friday," I said.

"Is it? I don't keep track."

"I get Friday and Saturday nights off."

The rototiller bucked, and the guy to the side who seemed to be coaxing the motor along yelled in Spanish at the guy who walked behind, steering. Anton and I listened. I didn't understand, but I think I got the gist. Job swearing.

"Come over," Anton said, eventually. "Wear that."

I glanced down at my tie. "My work clothes?"

"Yeah. Don't say anything. Just bust in and nail me, like a total badass."

"Hate to be a buzzkill, but I'm not a ba—"

The motor guy yelled—really yelled. I'd thought at first the rototiller had run him over. The steering guy reached around and cut the engine, and the motor guy's screaming filled the sudden silence.

"*¡El brazo! ¡El brazo!*"

I looked at Anton. He shrugged, then pushed away from the garage and strode over to see what the commotion was all about. I followed and veered over toward Melita to get a better handle on whatever was happening. "What's he saying?"

She hurried toward the rototiller with quick steps, but her legs were short and squat, and she started to fall behind. "An arm?"

The foreman was the first to reach the screaming man, who pointed to the ground and kept on screaming.

"It came up out of the ground," Melita translated, breathing hard.

The three landscapers crowded around the

front of the rototiller and spoke frantically, while Anton edged his way into their circle and peered at the soil. I didn't need to squeeze anyone aside. I could see right over the shortest landscaper's head.

The earth had churned up in huge chunks, brown on the surface, black underneath, filled with fibers, rocks and roots, and a few dangling earthworms. And down in the crevasse that the tiller had torn up, dirt crusted and grayish, fingers slightly furled, lay a human arm.

Chapter Eight

The sheriff and two deputies came to get a look at the arm. It turned out to be attached to a body. There was a lot of commotion. I did my best not to look. Anton looked so hard I think he went for an hour without blinking.

The landscapers were questioned and dismissed, and they looked pretty eager to leave. Anton stuck around. It seemed logical. His house bordered the same woods as the garden plot. He'd been there when we discovered the arm. But trying to talk to him was useless. He was so focused on that trench in the ground that trying to engage him in conversation was like talking to one of his sculptures.

Since I'd only set foot on the island for the first time a few days before, the sheriff talked to me for all of five minutes, mainly to get a sequence on the events in English that had led to the discovery. He moved on to Anton, and I turned toward the house to make sure the Whites were okay.

"Ray?"

I turned. One of the deputies looked at me expectantly.

"Yeah?"

He looked down at the paperwork the Sheriff had just handed him. "Ray Carlucci?"

Fucking-A. I had no idea the bill collectors' reach would extend out to Red Wing Island. "Yeah?"

"Ray from Body Art Studio, right?"

"Yeah." What good would it do to lie? They already had my name on record. "That was my shop."

"I got my first tattoo from you," he said. He was thirty, maybe. He turned and showed me the back of his windbreaker, pointed to his shoulder. "Right here. An eagle."

Cops and soldiers got eagles. A lot. I nodded and tried not let my relief show on my face.

"You probably don't remember.... Say, why'd you close the shop? Everyone I ever knew who ended up with an ugly tattoo from one of the other dives said they wished they'd gone to you instead."

"I retired." And because I was really in no mood to talk about Body Art Studio, I turned around and kept on walking, back to the house. Marnie stood by the window that looked out onto the yard. I don't think I had ever seen somebody literally wring their hands. She was doing that.

"Mrs. is upstairs with Mr. She's trying to keep him from getting upset. I think he knows something is going on, though. Go up there, Ray."

"I don't know what good it'll do...."

"Would it kill you to comfort them?"

Way to make me feel like a jerk. I went upstairs.

At the top of the stairs, I heard something fall and break. "Edgar...."

Shuffling. The sound of chair legs scraping on hardwood. I rounded the corner to the master bedroom and saw Mr. White grappling with his wife. He had her by the arms. I remember the feel of his fingers digging into the muscle of my forearm, and I stepped into the room without being asked, without even telling them that I was there.

"Hey, Mr. White. It's Ray. You probably don't remember me—I'm new. Mrs. White needs to go talk to some people. But you and me, we can hang out for a little while. What do you say? We can see what's on the radio. Or catch up on some talk shows."

"Raymond, what's happened?" said Mrs. White. "I don't understand."

I glanced at Mr. White. He didn't look like he was listening to me. But then again, according to him, Stanley never thought he'd been paying attention, and Stanley had been wrong.

"The landscapers found something in the yard. I think the sheriff will have to talk to you."

I encouraged Mr. White to sit in the armchair, turned on the radio, and found a station that wasn't playing news or advertisements. I sat beside him in a matching armchair, found the toothpick in my pocket, and gave the end of it a few good chews.

"You know Anton Kopec? He lives behind you. I wonder what you made of him—what would it have been? A few months ago? Or maybe you mostly knew his sister, before he came to live on the island."

Maybe Mr. White heard me and, in some part of his mind, understood. Or maybe not. We sat together and listened while the radio played smooth jazz.

Nearly an hour later, Marnie came upstairs. "They took him."

I thought I knew what she meant, but I hoped I was wrong. "Who took who?"

"The sheriff. He took Anton."

I looked at Marnie, hard. I wasn't sure what she expected me to say. "Did somebody call his sister?"

"He told me not to."

Mr. White shifted uneasily in his seat.

"Okay, they took him. And what?"

Marnie pulled me out into the hall and spoke in a whisper. "That was Stanley Marsh out there, our first driver. Anton recognized the buckle on a belt that the rototiller tore off the body."

"And because Anton spotted that, they think he put that guy in the ground?"

Marnie went over to the hall window, pushed aside the curtains, and gazed out over the tree-tops. "I don't know what they think. But what about you? Do you think he could do something like that?"

Actually, I didn't really know, and it unsettled me deep down inside. I'd thought Anton seemed okay—more than okay—but I'd been fooled by a pretty face before. Still. If he had buried Stanley in the yard, he'd been doing a damn good imper-sonation of someone who was more interested in my after-work plans than in what was going on around the rototiller. "I doubt it."

Once the deputies were through talking to Mrs. White, she asked me not to say anything to Edgar. I promised her I wouldn't. "We'll keep the floodlights on the house from now on after dark," she said. "If you don't mind looking out your window now and then, and making sure you don't see anyone in the yard...."

"You got it," I said. Marnie gave me a hunk of a frozen casserole to take back to the apartment over the garage. I was glad. I wanted some time to think without a bunch of frightened women contaminating me with their suspicions. I posi-tioned my small table in front of the window and stared out over the yard. Anton had said I looked like a thug playing dress-up. I'd thought he was teasing me. But what if there was a grain of truth in that? What if somebody at the White estate had been looking to hire a thug, and I fit the bill?

Marnie had said they wanted a man around the house—that I was supposed to be the muscle. I ate my microwaved leftovers without really tasting them. Maybe my sleeve *had* ridden up during the job interview, or maybe the missing button was more noticeable than I'd imagined. Maybe I really was a thug, albeit one who'd never seen himself that way.

The sheriff, the medical examiner, and the body were all gone by the time I finally turned off my light and crawled into bed. I stared at the ceiling, flinching at every rustle or noise, and it seemed as if I wouldn't sleep at all. Except I must have fallen asleep, because the sound of a phone ringing jolted me out of an uneasy slumber.

I turned on the light and cast around for the phone. I hadn't even known that there was a phone. An answering machine picked up before I found it.

"Hello, this is Gene. I'm not here, so leave a message after the beep." The sound of the second driver's voice gave me a start. I picked up a pile of kitchen towels next to the microwave and found a phone with a built-in answering machine beneath it. A couple of clicks, and then I heard:

"God damn it, Ray, you'd better fucking be there...."

I grabbed the receiver. "Anton?"

"Get me out of this fucking trailer they call a town hall, would you? The coffee fucking sucks."

"Okay. I'll be right there."

And I had no idea what I was really thinking when I promised him that, but I'd spoken before my brain was fully engaged. My work clothes were hung over the back of the chair, and I pulled them on, hoping that if I was wearing a tie, the deputies would be less likely to harass me for the bad loan. Even if I did look like a dressed-up thug.

It was after midnight, but Marnie and Melita were still awake when I rapped, low and urgent, on the kitchen door. "Can I borrow your car?" I whispered to Marnie.

She narrowed her eyes.

"Okay," I said. "I know you don't like him. But Anton needs a ride back to the island."

"I don't dislike him. It's just that he's got so many problems." She sighed and pulled a set of keys off the hook beside the door. "Take it. But hurry back, okay? Every little noise sounds like a murderer."

Marnie's car was a Subaru hatchback with four-wheel drive and a broken radio. I got a feel for the car on the narrow, pitch-dark roads of the island by the time I came to the bridge that led into town. The corrugated metal trailer that housed local utility payments, the local cops, and traffic court every other Tuesday had a squad car and two deputy's sedans in the parking lot. It was probably the most action the place had seen since the last election.

I opened the door and was bombarded by the sound of raised voices.

"...the phone number..."

"You want to talk to Diane so bad? Call her yourself. Or don't they teach you how to find a phone number on the Internet at the police academy?"

My gut sank. I knew that whatever I was walking into, it couldn't be good. I passed the dark window where people paid their utility bills and turned into the main room. Anton was pacing, and the flowing black-on-black that looked so fitting by moonlight was nowhere near as flattering in the green-tinged fluorescent of the town hall. Here, he looked like the type of nut job who'd bring a semiautomatic rifle to a shopping mall and let loose. The agitated pacing didn't help.

"Ray," he snapped, when he saw me. "I need to leave in the worst fucking way."

There were three deputies and two local cops standing around the perimeter of the room, all on high alert, though thank God, none of them had a weapon drawn. The deputy I'd talked to back at the Whites' house, the kid with the eagle tattoo, took a few cautious steps toward us. "Mr., uh, Carlucci? You okay to take him home? 'Cos we're prepared to hold him."

Anton stopped right in front of me, his face maybe a foot away from mine, and stared me in the face like he was trying to communicate with mental telepathy.

"Is he being charged with something?" I said. I kept my eyes on Anton. A sinew pulsed in his jaw where he clenched it.

"No, it's just.... I mean, we're trying to track down his sister."

Anton shook his head no so subtly I almost didn't see it.

"Don't bother. I'll drive him home."

Anton shoved past me, kicked open the front door, and burst out into the parking lot. I didn't linger behind and give the cops a reason to detain either of us.

By the time I got to the Subaru, he was on the opposite side of the car, repeatedly snapping the passenger door handle. I beeped the lock open, and he got in and slammed the door.

I got in and started the car. "You all right?" I said.

"No." He hugged the front of his coat to his chest and bounced his left knee.

I pulled out of the parking lot and onto the street. The closest window filled with deputies and cops, who watched us drive away.

"I take it you don't play well with law enforcement."

"Not when they fucking accuse me of fucking

killing my fucking friend."

"You and Stanley were friends?"

Anton shrugged sullenly. "I dunno. We hung out sometimes, when he scored weed."

Practically soul mates. I rolled my eyes, but I told myself to count to ten and not fan the flames. "They actually came out and said they thought you...."

"No, of course not. They can't. But stupid questions. Like whether I was screwing him. Whether maybe we had a lovers' quarrel."

I watched the road very carefully.

Anton pushed the seat all the way back and stretched out. "Whole thing's a fucking joke. You wanna stop at the bar and get me a six-pack? I'll pay you back."

"I don't have any cash on me."

"There's a cash station right inside the door."

I drove past the bar without slowing down. "Yeah. I don't have a debit card either."

I steeled myself for some of the abuse that the cops had been getting, but instead Anton started to laugh. "You mean you have no money? None at all? Zero?"

"Glad you find that so amusing."

He kept on laughing, an edgy sound, wild. "Oh, Ray...Ray of Moonlight. I'm not laughing at you." His head lolled on the headrest. I could see him staring at me in my peripheral vision. "Tell me you don't have a sister who suckered power of attorney out of you, then won't even give you the courtesy of a prepaid Visa card?"

"I don't have a sister," I said.

I saw him watching me as I drove, and I ignored him. They say that when you meet a guy, he'll tell you everything you need to know about him within the first five minutes. Johnny had spent the first five minutes gushing over my tats and my shop, which he eventually leached out from under me. Anton had asked me to build pyramids with him. And I believe he also mentioned that I'd think he was crazy.

"It freaked me out a little when I got Gene on the answering machine," Anton said. He seemed a lot calmer now. Maybe even normal, for him. "I remembered thinking I'd made you up, and for just a second there, back at the town hall, I had myself convinced that's what had really happened."

"I'm real, all right."

Anton put his hand on my thigh. "I'll say." Before I knew it, he'd slipped his fingers deep between my legs, far enough to cup my whole groin and slide his palm up and down.

The car swerved. I righted it. "Not the best time," I said.

He ignored me and manhandled my crotch. "You didn't give me any shit on the phone, you know that? You didn't make me explain or beg, or anything. I told you I needed you, and here you are. I called, you came."

I downshifted to first, then pulled over on the gravel shoulder. "There's probably a deputy tailing us to make sure I get you home." Or maybe to talk to me about a loan. Or both.

My cock was already stiffening. His fingers found the shape of it, glided up and down as it swelled and hardened. "Who said you should stop driving?"

"Anton...."

He launched himself at me, covered my mouth with his. I knew I shouldn't, but I let him suck my lower lip into his mouth, tease it with his tongue and teeth, while his hand stroked me through the dress slacks. His stubble was long enough to feel soft, and it tickled my upper lip. He smelled like turpentine and autumn leaves and coffee. And his hand, my God, his hand...it had me totally hard in a minute flat.

I turned my head to catch my breath, and my panting sounded harsh and close in the interior of the hatchback. "Don't jerk me off in Marnie's car." Because it was dark, and we were in a hurry, and if she saw or smelled or even sensed anything, I was sure I couldn't count on ever borrowing it again.

Anton nipped my jaw with his hot, wet mouth. His stubble whispered over my cheek. "Okay," he said.

He eased my fly down.

"I said...."

"Shh." He slid toward the passenger door, but only to make enough room to bend his head to my lap.

"Shit." I squeezed my eyes shut tight, hit the clutch, and jammed the shift into park under the weight of his upper body. I grabbed his long hair in my other fist. He coaxed my cock free from my slacks, and his mouth closed over it. Hot and wet. It was all I could think. Wet. So wet. So totally and utterly wet. He took me deep, gagged on it a little, then did it again, over and over. My cockhead squelched into the back of his throat. He sucked, hard, while he jacked the base with his fingers.

I held his head as it bobbed in my lap, and my fingers slid through his hair. I shouldn't. I thought those two words, over and over. I shouldn't. I shouldn't. Not in Marnie's car. Not on the side of the road at the edge of town, especially when the cops and the deputies were already looking at us sideways. Not without a condom.

Anton slurped his way up my cock, then licked his hand and polished the knob with his wet palm while he delved down low to slip his tongue into my fly and lick my balls.

I let out a shuddery breath, squeezed my right arm out from underneath his chest, and clutched his hair two-fisted. My hips rose to meet his strokes.

He tongued his way back up again, then swallowed my cock back down and deep-throated me while he toyed with my damp balls.

I thrust my hips—involuntary, almost a spasm—and Anton grunted his encouragement, sucked even more. I grabbed his head hard, and he gave a long, low moan. The noise warbled in his throat, because my cock was sinking in and out of it. I was close, so close I didn't care anymore. I pulled his hair, jammed his head down against my lap, and flicked my hips up to bury myself deep.

Wet, so wet...and I was gagging him, and I didn't give a damn, because all I cared about was coming in that irresistible, hot, wet mouth.

The first spurt was halfway there when I realized I was peaking, and I tried to pull Anton back. He ignored me, sucked me even harder, brutal and demanding. My cock pulsed in his mouth, and he sucked and sucked, until finally my hips stopped moving and I stopped making that strangled, fatalistic sound.

The bobbing of his head slowed and grew still, and he pulled off without any hurry, pausing to kiss the shaft and the glans. The sound of his lips smacking against my cock was wet and loud in the dark interior of the car.

He pushed up, stroked the front of my shirt, my tie, and then pressed his mouth to mine. His mouth was sticky and hot, and his lips felt swollen. I tasted my come on his kiss.

Chapter Nine

An overly cheerful doorbell woke me the next morning, and I wondered how many ways there were, in that three-room apartment of mine, that someone could wake me up without my prior consent. "I'm coming," I yelled, though I suspected that it probably didn't carry all the way down to the door on the side of the garage, and in a passive-aggressive sort of way, I didn't care.

I pulled on last night's slacks and dress shirt, left my feet bare and the buttons on the shirt undone, and dragged my ass to the bottom of the stairs. A deputy as big as me filled my doorway, khaki uniform and mirrored cop shades. The sun slanted into my eyes from behind him, just risen and brutal, and the grass and leaves glittered with frost. Here we go, I thought. Here's where I go down for that fucking loan.

"Sorry to wake you, Mr. Carlucci." The deputy didn't sound all that sorry. I waited for whatever words would come before he hauled me off. "We found something in the woods, and we wondered if you might be able to shed some light on it."

Woods. He wasn't there about the loan, after all. "Depends on what that something is."

He turned back toward the tree line. Sunlight glanced off the silver frame of his shades. He grimaced. His teeth were large and very white. "Someone's been monkeying around in the old burial plot."

I stuck my forefinger and thumb into my eyes and pinched out the sandy residue of sleep, and wondered if he could've possibly just said what I'd just heard him say. It seemed as far-out as, "...and developers built the place on an ancient Navajo burial ground." And not much better than, "I'm here to see you about a debt."

"Define *monkeying around*."

"Branches stacked around the headstones, tied off at the top."

Relief and revulsion flooded me at the same time. Relief, because I'd imagined grave robbing, or worse. But headstones? Jesus. "They're some kind of modern art...thing," I said. "I don't really get it."

The deputy's shoulders relaxed, and he nodded. "So it's Kopec."

"Yeah. An installation piece, I think. Something about pyramids."

"Takes all kinds, I guess. I hear his work sells in Detroit."

"I've heard that too."

"All right then. We'll let you know if we need anything else."

No doubt. I closed the door, went back upstairs, and got dressed. I'd figured I'd be less likely to be singled out by the cops if I did my best to blend in as one of the staff.

I went into the house and walked right into another "accident" of Mr. White's that left me bruised and soaked to the skin. As I held him steady in the shower, his eyes were totally vacant, and I wondered how it was possible that the part of himself that had spoken to me just a few nights ago could just completely and utterly vanish.

I ate my lunch at the kitchen table. Marnie moved around the kitchen a lot more forcefully than she needed to, and she banged things around the cupboards as she emptied the dishwasher.

"What?" I said finally.

She planted her hands on her hips and looked out the window over the sink. "We haven't said anything to Mr.," she told me, "but I swear, it's as if he knows. And he's upset, which is making him worse."

"I think he sees more than we know. Or maybe he picks up on our body language." Or maybe it was just the progression of his Alzheimer's.

Marnie pulled out a chair and sat down hard. "Yeah. Something like that." She planted her elbow on the table and put her face in her hand. "What are we gonna do, Ray?"

"Maybe it's time for them to look into a nursing home."

She sat back and combed her graying hair from her forehead with her fingertips. I did my best not to think about running my fingers through Anton's hair while he sucked me off.

"Mr.'s brother went into a nursing home—a ritzy one too—and he was dead within a month. He'd been spitting out his high blood pressure pills. No one noticed."

I wasn't exactly an authority on eldercare, so I wasn't going to argue with her. "Have you met Anton's sister?"

"Sure. Why?"

"He said she had power of attorney over him."

Marnie nodded to herself. It looked like there was a lot she knew, but she was picking and choosing her words carefully. "I guess she didn't want to keep him in a home any more than we want to put Mr. White away."

I steeled myself for something bad. "So what's his deal? Schizophrenic?"

"Bipolar. I've never seen him depressed, though, not in the traditional sense of the word. Usually he cycles between up and really up. Sometimes when I hear him working at night, I wonder if he even sleeps during the day, or he just keeps going."

"Everyone says his artwork sells. Why doesn't

he have any money?"

"He spends it, I guess. The second it's in his hand, it's as good as gone. So Diane makes sure he has a place to live, has food and medications delivered every week, and she knows he's okay. As okay as he'll ever be."

We both stared at the table for a minute or two. "You think he killed Stanley?" I asked.

She toyed with her coffee cup. "Last night, when the police were digging in the yard, I had myself convinced that he'd done it. But you seemed so sure he hadn't, and the more I thought about it, the more I realized that even if he had— let's say, by accident, they fought about something and it got out of hand—that I don't think he'd be able to cover it up and just forget about it, act like nothing had happened."

Not exactly a glowing recommendation of Anton's mental state. But probably pretty accurate.

Mrs. White came into the kitchen dressed in a lavender sweater set, low-heeled pumps, and pearls. Her skin looked gray underneath her rouge. I wondered when the last time was she'd slept more than a couple of hours at a stretch. "Your paychecks," she said and handed Marnie and me each an envelope. "I'd meant to give them to you yesterday, but all the excitement...."

"We understand," Marnie said. "Don't worry about it."

I nodded my understanding and had to restrain

myself from tearing open the envelope and rubbing the paycheck all over my body in an uninhibited display of relief.

Melita followed with a vase of drooping flowers. She stuffed the flowers into the trash and dumped the water in the sink. "You got a bank account, Ray?"

"Not...currently."

"Drive me into town, and I'll let you sign the check over to me so you can cash it."

"That's a wonderful idea," said Mrs. White. "The bank closes at three on Saturday. I feel terrible that you didn't get your night off. Why don't you take the Town Car?"

Melita and I didn't have anything to say to each other on the way to the bank. We got there right before they closed. The teller informed me that I could open my very own checking account with a deposit of as little as fifty dollars, plus fourteen fifty for checks. Since my three days' salary minus tax had come out to less than two hundred bucks, and especially since I had no desire to leave my new address so that bill collectors could start hounding me again, I declined.

Melita and I made our way back in silence, until she pointed to a tiny strip mall at the edge of town. "Turn in there." The mall contained a car wash, a liquor store, and a tax preparation office, which was closed.

"You went through all this so you could get

some booze?" I said.

"What do you mean, 'all this'? I wanted to get out of that house for a few minutes, that's all." Melita went into the liquor store and came back out stuffing a pint into her big vinyl purse.

She pulled the car door shut and clasped her purse on her lap. "Don't say nothing, all right? I had trouble sleeping last night. I kept thinking about that hand in the ground."

The dirt-crusted nails sprang to mind. I shuddered. "Nobody's business but your own," I said. "And thanks for cashing my check."

"Eh, *de nada*." We drove down the winding tree-lined road, and I squirmed as I passed the shoulder where I'd pulled over the night before.

"I'm glad it was Stanley," Melita said, out of nowhere.

I glanced at her.

"I mean, him and not Gene. Stanley was kind of an asshole. Gene was quiet. Didn't bother me."

That was the opposite of what I'd heard so far about the previous drivers. Stanley had been Anton's friend—friendly enough to smoke pot together, anyway—and Gene had made Marnie uncomfortable by putting the moves on her.

"Last Christmas was the worst," she said. "Mr. White gave me a nice bonus, 'cos I'd been there ten years. I wasn't bragging or nothing. I just thought it was a nice thing for him to do, and Marnie did too. But Stanley, he got all crazy.

Jealous. I had Marnie drive me straight to the bank, put the whole check in, all but twenty dollars."

We bumped over the narrow bridge, turned onto the winding road that led to the house.

"After that, Stanley was always nasty to me, made a point of complaining about the way I did this or that." She clucked her tongue. "I thought when he left, he'd come back eventually. Maybe he met some new girl in town, went on a drinking binge with her. Tried to show everyone how bad we needed him by staying away. But Mrs. White must've figured out that he wasn't coming back. She started looking right away, found Gene."

"Seems like it should've been Gene buried in the yard," I said.

Melita looked at me sharply.

"I mean, if Stanley's an asshole, and he takes off to prove how valuable he is, and instead Mrs. White replaces him right away with Gene. And then Gene disappears...."

Melita nodded. "Yeah, and I wouldn't put it past Stanley neither. But Mr. Kopec could tell one from the other. You'd never mix up the two of them, even if they was dead awhile." She sketched a big belly in the air, all the way out to the dashboard. "Gene was fat. And besides, there was that belt buckle."

I dropped Melita off at the house with her secret stash and told her I was going for a walk, and that I had my two-way radio on me.

A pair of crime scene techs were still process-ing the spot where they'd dug up Stanley Marsh. I went around to the front of the house to get some distance between them and me, and then I slipped into the tree line that divided the Whites' property and Anton's place.

I was chilled within minutes and wished I'd helped myself to one of Gene's sport coats, whether it fit me or not. The woods seemed larger during the day, as if by seeing the depth and breadth of the rows of trees, I couldn't fool myself into thinking that it would just be a few more steps before I emerged into a clearing.

I wove through trees, decided that I was well and truly lost, then reassured myself that the island just wasn't that big and that eventually I was bound to come out on either the road or some wealthy snowbird's backyard.

Once I finally broke through, I found myself in the hollow where I'd first met Anton. Four branch-pyramids stood at the opposite end of the long, narrow clearing. They were only heaps of sticks and twine, I told myself. Nothing more. But the way they hulked together, like a herd of lumbering beasts, filled me with a vague revul-sion. My dress shirt pulled across my shoulders and throat like it would suffocate me. I loosened my tie, rolled my shoulders, and approached the pyramids.

Sticks and twine. So why did they feel so ominous?

I parted the dried leaves that still clung to the branches and looked inside. There, in the center, was a stone slab that I would've taken for a cast-off cinder block, especially in the dark. Except now the deputy's words rang in my head: old burial plot.

Headstones.

Pyramids, Rosicrucians, and graves. I probably didn't want to know what Anton's "experiment" was all about—but I was hoping there was some thread of logic in it that a person might be able to follow, even if he was just marginally sane.

I thought about banging on Anton's door, demanding to know what he was trying to prove by lurking around the woods at night and building tepees on people's graves, but I decided not to. Either I'd end up having to admit to myself just how screwed up he really was, or he'd manage to sidetrack me with his hands and mouth and cock so that I'd forget what explanation I'd gone there for to begin with.

I ducked into the woods again and made my way back toward the Whites' property. The phone in my apartment had a caller ID readout. Nobody ever cleared those things. I'd look back on that, see if there was a call left over from Stanley's days. Anton had known the number by heart, so obviously he'd called it before, frequently. I could get him on the phone and see what he had to say for himself, without the distraction of his mouth on mine and his hand down my pants.

I pushed aside a thick tangle of branches and shrubs and stepped out into what I thought would be the Whites' expansive front yard. Except a tall chain-link fence stretched in front of me. A metal sign was riveted about five and a half feet off the ground, and it repeated every few yards. *Private Property – Protected by Huron Security*.

Great. The survivalist's house.

Chapter Ten

I tried to picture the lay of the roads and orient myself. I'd veered around in an arc, somehow. I followed the chain link until it ended at the back corner of the property, then abutted the spike-topped wrought iron that encircled the rest of the house. I adjusted my course, and made my way, eventually, back to the Whites' property.

At that point, the nip in the air had gone way beyond the point where I could call it that. I saw my breath, strikingly white, with every exhalation. And I was so cold that by the time I finally did wander out into the right clearing, I'd been chewing on stories about people who get lost in the snow and lie down in a drift and simply fall asleep as hypothermia takes them.

The kitchen door was locked. I banged on it, and Marnie let me in. "Look at you—you're all red. How long have you been outside without a coat on?"

"I got a little turned around in the woods."

"Go sit down. I'll get you something hot. Coffee?

Tea?"

"Coffee, black, one sugar."

The top of the kitchen table was clear, save for a single key and a blurred digital photo printed on plain white paper. The photo had been taken right there in the kitchen, a shot of a guy who needed a haircut, in a shirt and tie. "Stanley?" I guessed, because he didn't look portly enough to be Gene.

Marnie nodded. "There's his key. You should take it. We'd feel better knowing you can come in even if we're locked down for the night."

"Or the day," I said.

She put a cup of coffee in front of me, pulled out a chair, and sat down. "I know that they don't have enough police to keep anyone on the island, especially since Stan's probably been dead for a while and whoever killed him is long gone. But I wish they could leave someone here anyway."

I pulled out my keys and tried to pry open the ring and slide the house key on. My fingers were bright red, and they stung like a bitch.

"Here, you have frostnip." Marnie took my keys and slid the new key onto the ring.

I nodded. I should've worn my leather jacket, on duty or not. I'd misestimated the depth and breadth of the woods. "When did it get to be winter all of a sudden?"

"Gets worse every year, doesn't it? They're saying record lows tonight, in the single digits.

You'll need to dig out the area between the house and the garage if it snows. A plow comes from town to do the driveway...and you usually have to dig out the garage door again once they're done. Snowblower, rock salt, and shovels are on the right side of the garage."

I hadn't shoveled snow in ages, but I suspected it didn't take a PhD to clear a driveway. I hoped it did snow. At least shoveling it would help me take my mind off Stanley's body in the rototiller trench.

I holed myself up in the apartment above the garage, layered on Gene's old sweatshirts, and drank cup after cup of instant decaf thick with sugar until finally I felt warm again, though my stomach didn't care much for the faux joe. I listened to the clock radio for a while, but the severe weather warnings started to outnumber the songs, which all sucked, and also made me miss the CD collection I'd sold to pay off a creditor who never appreciated it anyway. Digging through the recycle bin yielded some relatively fresh newspapers. I caught up on the state of world affairs; then I tore out every crossword puzzle I could find. I turned in somewhere around an eight-letter word for apex.

The bed still smelled strange, like the apartment. Not lived-in enough to smell like me, yet. I pulled the covers up to my chin and listened to the wind howl while hail pelted the roof, and tree branches scritched across my bathroom windowpane. And I wondered what the storm sounded like from Anton's house.

I slept and was woken by Marnie's voice on the intercom. "Ray? Are you there?"

Where else would I be? That was the first reply that sprang to mind. Though since I hadn't mentioned how edgy Anton had been acting when I picked him up at the town hall, I could see her thinking that maybe I'd decided to wait out the storm in his sister's guesthouse. After all, it had technically been my night off.

I pressed the button. "Yeah."

"It's a sheet of ice outside. I need you to spread salt to the end of the driveway."

It was still dark out. I looked at the clock. Six thirty—practically the middle of the night. But I didn't complain about it. I'd been itching for something to do.

I layered hand-me-down sweatshirts under my leather jacket, then went out and started spreading salt. Marnie hadn't been exaggerating when she said it was a sheet of ice out there. I could have played hockey on the driveway.

Not only that, but the whole world was glazed with at least a half inch of ice—the grass, the rooftops, and weirdest of all, the trees. The autumn leaves that hadn't gotten a chance to fall looked candy-coated, and the branches drooped low under the weight of all the ice.

It was beautiful, in an eerie, surreal kind of way. Anton was probably loving it. Unless he thought it was the work of aliens. Or Rosicrucians.

The first overburdened tree went down as I was looking in the general direction of Anton's place and trying to figure out what sorts of things went on inside his head. It was loud. Leaves that had once rustled together now made a weird, dull clatter, and the roots snapped as they tore from the sandy soil. It left an indentation in the tree line of the woods that separated the two properties.

Once the tree was on its side, everything was quiet again except the constant patter of hail.

I took a few steps toward the kitchen door and slid. I decided it might be better to stay put and try out my two-way radio instead. It was tuned to channel twelve already. "Marnie?" I called. No answer. I headed carefully for the house and let myself in with the key.

"Marnie?"

She was elbow-deep in dough. "What was that noise?"

"A tree fell. It was so full of ice it just tore up out of the ground. I tried to call you on the two-way."

"Oh. Right. It helps to turn it on and have it near you, doesn't it? Gene was the only one who ever seemed to remember it. I'll dig it out, just as soon as...."

"No big deal." I poured some coffee, and looked

out the window at the gray of the gradually light-
ening sky against the silhouette of the glassy
treetops. The wind howled, and hail clattered on
the windowpane. And then I heard the clattery
rustle turn into a series of ominous snaps. A gap
appeared in the tree line. "Damn. Another one."

I craned my neck as if I could see Anton's
house from there. Which, of course, I couldn't.

"Call him," Marnie said—and maybe she
sounded a little resigned, like she knew I was a
goner when it came to that man, and there was
nothing she could say that would change it. But
I was glad she'd suggested checking on him to
make sure he hadn't been flattened by an ice-
covered tree. I turned and looked at her. She was
forming the dough into rows of tiny crescents.
She indicated the phone with her head. "He's on
memory dial. I forget which. Just look at the list."

I picked up the phone. "Do I have to hit nine
to dial out?"

"No, just memory dial, then the number."

There was no dial tone. I followed her instruc-
tions anyway. The phone dialed a Mr. Kopec,
memory dial six, but nothing happened other
than the quick series of seven touch tones.

"I don't have an outside line."

"What do you mean? It's automatic." She put
down her dough, took the phone from me with
a kitchen towel–covered hand, and wedged the
handset between her shoulder and cheek. "Damn.

The phone's out."

I glanced at the window. A gust of wind peppered the glass with hail, and the trees gave off their clattery rustle. "Maybe I should check."

"Anything happens to Mr., I'd need you to drive."

"The roads are beyond slick. Your Subaru's gonna handle the ice better than the Town Car ever could." And who else would check on Anton, if not me? His sister, wherever she was?

Marnie thought for several long seconds. "Make it fast," she said, finally. "Get him to come back here if you can. It'll be safer here than in that dinky house of his."

We tested the two-way radios, then I set off for Anton's. Even the grass was slippery, and it was slow moving until I got to the woods, where the tree canopy had caught the ice before it hit the ground.

I hadn't been prepared for the sound of the creaking. It surrounded me. And the thought that once of those monster maples could uproot and flatten me scared me shitless.

I hurried through the clearing, overcompensated, and ended up in the backyard of Anton's next-door neighbor. A tall row of privacy shrubs separated the properties. Who knows what I expected to see when I rounded the bushes. Anton, surrounded by a hundred glasses, bowls, and jars? Not that.

But there he was, catching hail with the delight

of a child gathering fireflies. His hair was plastered to his forehead and cheeks, and his long black coat caught the wind like a sail as he moved from one container to the next, adjusting them as if their position made any difference one way or the other.

"Anton," I said. I could've asked him what he was doing, but really, did I need to know? He was in his zone, and whatever it might be, it undoubtedly made perfect sense to him.

And, I realized with no small amount of envy, maybe I'd rather be catching hailstones than salting a driveway, myself.

"Ray!" He straightened up, beaming. Ice glinted off the ends of his hair. He'd shaved. His smooth, pale cheeks looked gaunt and vulnerable, and his disarming smile seemed wider. He held his arms out as if to encompass the newly glazed world. "Look."

I approached him through the obstacle course of glasses and jars.

"It's really you, Ray, isn't it?"

"As opposed to...?"

"I don't know, I had a wild night. Talked to Stanley for a while. I asked him if he wanted me to build a pyramid over his grave. He said I'd better wait until the cops are done poking around."

"Real Stanley or metaphorical Stanley?"

"Reality is relative, isn't it?" He poked at a large

hailstone inside the glass he held. "But since he's dead, it must have been the Stanley in my mind."

At least he knew the difference. Kind of. "Phones are out."

He looked at me oddly, as if he couldn't imagine why it would matter. When I got close enough, he dropped the glass, took my face two-handed, pulled me up against him, and kissed me. He smelled like winter.

I turned away reluctantly. "It's not safe outside," I said. "Trees are falling left and right; they can't take the weight of all the ice."

"I've never known anyone to succumb to death by hardwood, have you?"

"And I don't want you to be the first. Come back with me."

Anton looked up at the sky. Hail, and now a bit of snow, dusted his cheeks, caught in his black eyebrows and lashes. "Nothing will happen to me."

"Come on, I haven't got time to argue. I came and got you last night, right? So you owe me one. Come back with me, so I don't have to worry."

He cupped my cheek with his palm and cocked his head. "You'd worry about me? You don't strike me as the type, all tattoos and macho." He looked down, gazed longingly at his glasses and jars, then shrugged. "Okay. I suppose I can hang out at the Whites' for a while."

He took me by the hand and started toward

the tree line. He didn't bother to lock his door, and I decided I was better off not compromising whatever momentum we had by suggesting that he should. He slid on an iced-over patch of leaves, and I hauled him up by the arm. He laughed and went even faster. And I realized I felt alive when I was with him. Maybe not always in a good way. Sometimes I was spooked, and sometimes I could smack him. But whatever was going on inside me, when we were together, good or bad— it was always vivid.

An ominous cracking sounded to one side of us, and a massive, ice-laden branch came crashing down. Anton yanked my arm and dragged me into the woods.

"Maybe we should've taken the road."

He answered me breathlessly, not with fear, but excitement. "It's ten times longer—and besides, the trees are just as thick."

Anton knew the woods. We came upon the clearing in minutes and found ourselves surrounded by seven-foot-tall branch pyramids. The forest floor was wet but not icy, so we technically didn't need to keep holding on to each other, but I didn't let go of Anton's hand, and he didn't let go of mine.

"Could you imagine how they would've looked with ice?" he said as we passed them.

I could. Creepier still.

"This way," he told me, and although I didn't

have the firmest grasp of direction in that clearing, I did recognize the gap that had led me to the survivalist's house the last time I'd been there.

"That's the wrong way."

"I'm not lost—I just want to see something quick."

"Seriously, I gotta get back. They're all spooked about the weather...and about Stanley."

"Trust me, Ray. It'll take two minutes."

Anton ducked through the gap first, then hauled me after, but instead of taking the obvious path that I'd taken the time I got lost, he sidestepped into a smaller gap and dragged me along behind him.

I was so busy waving annoying branches away from my face that I didn't see the smaller clearing until we were in the middle of it. This one was bright with diffuse gray light, as the canopy above didn't quite cover it. "I was hoping there'd be more ice," Anton said, looking up.

I followed his gaze. The entire clearing was surrounded by a giant web. Its strands were thick and utilitarian—a web of twine. Sections of the twine glittered with ice and frost, and in those spots, it was magical. "I did this last night," Anton said, "when I heard the storm was coming."

We ducked under a hub of crossed twine. He led me over to an area where the ice had coated everything thickly. "Wouldn't it be cool if it all looked like this?"

"You got a camera?"

Anton petted my cheek. "You fail to see the point, although I'm not really surprised. After all, everything you do is permanent. As permanent as frail mortality, anyway." He let go of my hand, opened his arms, and spun around. "We've seen it. That's enough."

I'll bet his sister would have a great time trying to sell that to a gallery. I followed one of the glittering lines, saw it cross another spoke of the web, head over to a branch, wrap it, then go off in another direction. I couldn't imagine how much twine he'd gone through. It must've taken him hours.

Everything was crooked, intriguingly asymmetrical. I decided that I liked the way the frost had hit portions of the web but not others. I found myself rotating in circles too, so I could take in the whole thing.

And then I spotted the part where something had broken free, and dangling tails of snapped twine swayed in the wind.

"Whatever you were trying to catch? I think it escaped." I pointed at the hole.

Anton darted over to the ruined section. He didn't seem angry at all. Actually, I'd say he was fascinated. "Now, what on earth would be tall enough to snap these lines?"

I felt a chill that had nothing to do with the cold wind blowing down the back of my neck.

"Okay, I saw your web. Let's go back to the house."

"This is five and a half feet off the ground. What do you think, are there bears on the island?"

"That's not funny."

"Depends on your sense of humor—take yours, for instance. I thought it was a little sicker. But don't worry, I'll bring you around to my point of view, eventually. Okay, it probably wasn't a bear. A bear would be walking on all fours, and he would've gone right underneath. So it must've been a human."

"You said there wasn't anyone on the island but us."

"Did I? No, what I said was that security was tight and that my count was off. And what good's the security, anyway? You need electricity to run the burglar alarms."

"The phones are out, not the electricity."

"Really? I haven't had power since midnight."

God damn. "Come on. I need to get back."

I imagine he heard me, but he felt no need to pay attention. He stepped through the gap in the trees that was surrounded by dangling twine. I followed. Not eagerly, but I followed.

I came through the trees yet again on the survivalist's property, this time at the opposite corner from the one I'd visited before. Anton was busy squeezing through a gap between the chain link and the wrought-iron fence. "What are you doing?" I said.

"This fence used to be tight. Somebody's been here before. Don't you want to take a look?"

Not particularly. I hadn't signed on for that. "I need to get back to the Whites. Are you coming or not?"

"Go." He made a shooing motion with his hand. "I'll be right behind you.... Hey, I see a footprint." He crouched and ran his fingers along the ground.

Right, as if I could turn around and not look. I tried to slip through the gap in the fence. I was too big to just cram myself through. I bent the chain link back, and it took a lot of squeezing and swearing, but finally, I made it.

"Someone must have walked through right before the ground froze." Anton pointed at a very distinct footprint. "See?"

"Hey." I caught his hand, held it between mine. "We shouldn't be messing around here. We should tell the police."

Anton raised my hand to his mouth and kissed each of my knuckles. The feel of his mouth tugged at my memory, and I imagined it closing around my cock. "The police?" he said. "I'm tempted to do just the opposite. I hate those pricks. But for you? Maybe...for you."

I turned back toward the gap in the fence, meaning to leave. But then I took one last look at the footprint, except then I saw another footprint, and another, and then I saw an old-fashioned tornado door where the footprints obviously led.

I pointed. "There. That's where they go."

"Seriously, Ray, how can you want to leave now?"

"Easy. I want to keep myself in one piece."

"You know how Stanley died? He was strangled. That's what those dumbfucks at the town hall told me. Actually, they suggested that maybe I strangled him when that supposed lovers' quarrel of ours went a little too far. Do you think the murderer's going to pop out and instantaneously strangle you? I think between the two of us we can overpower a single unarmed guy."

Just because the killer strangled Stanley didn't mean he didn't have a gun. Maybe he'd just been trying to be quiet. "No, no way."

I went into my own pocket and pulled out the two-way radio. I figured I would call Marnie, see if there was a channel the police monitored, if the range was long enough to reach town—or at least see if our phone was working again. Mainly I wanted the opinion of someone who wasn't gung-ho to follow a set of frozen footprints.

By the time I wrestled it out of my pocket, Anton had the cellar doors open. "You think I'm kidding around?" I said. I grabbed a handful of his coat, pulled him back. I spoke into his ear. "This is real, Anton. This is dangerous."

He turned his head, and the frozen tips of his hair brushed my jaw. "Life is dangerous." He was so eager to press on, I felt like I was straining to hold back a greyhound at the starting gate.

"Before you go in there, tell me. If Stanley left the Whites' suddenly, how come Marnie just gave me his key? Shouldn't it have been in his pocket?"

Anton stopped straining against my grip. "He always had his keys. He always locked his door. And I learned fast to call before I dropped over, since he'd blow a fuse if I just swung by and rang the doorbell."

"So where'd they get his keys?"

Anton turned away from the slanted doors that led beneath the survivalist's home, and he grabbed my leather jacket by both lapels so he could talk right in my face. "You saying one of them killed him? It would make for a titillating story around the bonfire, but come on. Whodunnit—Mrs. White, in the conservatory, with a figurine?"

"Remember the finger marks on my arm?"

"The spiderweb–cloud dragon arm, or the tiger–eight ball arm?"

"Never mind. How about this? What if Mr. White finds Stanley poking around, doing something he isn't supposed to be doing, and goes after him. Mr. White's still strong. Stanley wouldn't have expected it; he would've never known what hit him. Afterward, Mr. White forgets all about what he did, but Mrs. White needs to cover it up, or else it's institution time for her husband. So she hires Gene to get rid of the body, then pays him off so he leaves and never tells anyone."

"Hey, that really would make a much cooler campfire tale than I thought, especially if you work on the delivery, build up the suspense, tell it in a creepier voice." Anton pressed his forehead to mine. The icy tips of his hair tickled my cheek. "So if Mr. White's the killer, then we've got nothing to worry about, and you don't have to keep trying to stop me from having a look at whatever Harlan Scott keeps underneath his house. 'Cos it's bound to be good."

He broke away from me, black overcoat billowing as he spun, and disappeared down the cellar door—and no amount of tugging, coaxing, or threatening to leave had even the slightest effect on his trajectory.

My idea did make sense. But it didn't explain who'd been in Scott's basement when the ice storm hit. I took a few steps down, then crouched to see what I could. The cellar was black, with a single flashlight beam flickering around. "Anton," I whispered.

"Grab a flashlight." He sounded disturbingly nonchalant. "There's like five of them on a charging station at the foot of the stairs."

I held on for dear life as I crept the rest of the way down. Who knew that navigating a narrow staircase in the dark would feel like walking a tightrope? A motor chugged a few yards away from me, hard to tell exactly what kind, in the dark. I found the table, groped, and pulled one of the flashlights from it. I turned it on, and afterimages danced in front of my eyes, which had already adjusted to the suffocating darkness. I swung the beam toward the noise. It landed on a generator—a generator inside a padlocked metal cage. "Anton?"

"There's a bed down here." His voice wasn't far from me, but I couldn't find him with my flashlight beam. Too much black. "You should throw me down on it, show me who's boss."

"We just broke into your neighbor's house."

"The door was open. No harm, no foul. C'mon, Ray, you know you wanna. You said no back in the car too...then you jammed your cock in my mouth and held my head down while you came."

"I wasn't thinking."

"Thinking's overrated. I've jerked off three, four times remembering the way your hands felt on my head when you shot your load and forced me to swallow it."

I've never forced anyone to do anything... although I had been holding his head awfully hard, and I damn well knew it. I closed my eyes and tried to imagine something that would get me out of the cellar, and out of the conversation too. "What if the police come back and check this place out? Now it's full of your fingerprints, my fingerprints. Come on, let's go. Come back to the Whites' house for now and then spend the night with me."

Anton was already done talking. His flashlight beam flickered over a bank of supplies, cans and bottles and cartons. "Jackpot." I saw the red-labeled vodka bottles spotlighted by his flashlight beam as clearly as if they'd been on display at the liquor store. He tucked a single bottle into his coat. "Okay, now we can go."

"You came here looking for booze? Jesus Christ, Anton. Who knows what could've been down here."

"A bed...."

"And you're stealing. Have you thought of that?"

"Oh, please, don't be so melodramatic—it doesn't fit with your whole thug image. I'll totally pay him for it. I'm sure Diane will let some cash trickle down before he comes back next spring."

"Okay, that's it." I groped around the buttons on my two-way radio with my thumb until I pressed the key that lit them all up, and then I made sure I was on channel twelve. "Hello, Marnie?"

A crackle sounded on the far end of the cellar, and my own voice echoed back, a fraction of a second after I spoke. It was strange and indistinct, nearly drowned out by the chug of the generator. But I'd heard it.

I froze. I could feel my heart beating in my throat. Even Anton was still.

I put the radio to my mouth. "Hello?"

The word repeated, overlapping itself slightly.

Hell-hello.

"Now, this," Anton whispered, "this is a much cooler story than Mrs. White in the conservatory."

"Shine your flashlight over there," I snapped. I aimed my beam with one hand, held the radio to my mouth with the other.

"Hell-hello. Hell-hello."

A couple of burlap sacks were pushed against the corner. Flour, potatoes...who knows? But something leaned among them that obviously didn't belong—a seated figure, covered by an old army blanket. A man, judging by the feet sticking out from the edge of the blanket. Or maybe, more accurately, a body, because it seemed too still to call it a man.

I talked into the radio.

Hell-hello.

Anton covered the distance to the body in a few long strides.

"Don't touch it...."

I spoke too late, not that anything I said would have stopped him. He whisked the blanket off, then gave a low whistle. "You should ask for a raise. Your job is a lot more dangerous than it's cracked up to be."

Marnie'd said that Gene always kept his radio on him. "I'm wearing his clothes," I said, because my brain seemed to be stuck on that single, seemingly insignificant point. Not how he'd gotten there, or worse, how he'd died. Just the clothes.

Some kind of coping mechanism on my part, I guess.

"I went my whole life without ever seeing a corpse," Anton said, fascinated. "Outside of a funeral home, of course, which doesn't count because it's such an artificial construct—ritualized and sanitized. Now it's two in the same week. Maybe I *should* have brought my camera."

"We're getting out of here." I grabbed Anton by the arm, and he let me haul him back to the narrow stairs. "Go." I shoved him ahead of me, because I didn't trust him not to wander back while I climbed out.

Stanley, Gene, and now me. That would be the logical progression, wouldn't it? The blood and guts outside my front door hadn't been left there by a stray cat. They'd been a warning. Get out—while you still can.

And now I was stuck on the island until the plows made it over the bridge with their salt spreaders, or the weather turned—and judging by the sound of hail pinging off the cellar door, that wasn't happening anytime soon.

Anton cleared the top stair. "Stanley," he said.

"What about him?"

Anton hadn't been speaking to me, however, because another voice answered him. "Go home. You don't need to see this."

"Come back when I'm not with Ray, okay? I'm trying to make a good impression here—and talking to dead people in front of him won't help."

I climbed out of the tornado cellar and found Anton having a conversation with a guy who definitely wasn't dead—particularly in the way he was holding a shotgun. His hair was longer than it had been in Marnie's photo, he'd grown a patchy beard, and his clothes looked ragged and disheveled—like he'd been living in someone's basement for God-knows-how-long. But he was far from dead.

I'd never met Harlan Scott, but I was guessing he wouldn't have taken kindly to a stranger living in his basement. I also suspected he hadn't left the island early for winter after all, and that he'd been napping under the Whites' garden plot for quite a while, with Stanley's belt, the thing that had strangled him, alongside his body, waiting to catch on the rototiller blade. Once the medical examiner ran dental records or fingerprints, we'd know for sure.

No doubt the man we were facing would've loved to have stayed upstairs in Scott's house, with a shower and a satellite TV. But he probably hadn't counted on the locked generator keeping the alarm system running. "So," I said, doing my best to sound casual. "You're Stanley."

Stanley pumped the shotgun. The sound rang through the iced-over yard like a snapping tree branch. He aimed at me. "And you're living in my house."

Anton had gone his whole life without ever seeing a corpse? I'd gone mine without ever having a shotgun pointed at my head. My hands rose of their own accord, as if to say, *You wouldn't shoot an unarmed man, would you?* "Hey, look, it's just a job, okay? You want it back, you got it."

"Just a job." He laughed, an ugly little bark. "Edgar have one of his 'accidents' yet? How'd you like cleaning that up?"

Anton grabbed Stanley's elbow. "Don't point that thing at Ray."

Stanley yanked his arm free. I watched the shotgun barrel leap, and I wondered just how sensitive the trigger was. "You know how long I give Edgar?" he said. "A year, if that. Once old guys start losing it, they slide, fast. And his wife never had kids, never had a job. All she had was him. So my guess is, once he's gone, she's not far behind."

Was there some way to un-pump a shotgun? I didn't know. I'd never touched one, myself. "Why don't you just put that thing down...?"

"That property, that car, all that fucking money. And no kids. Think about it. No kids."

"Put the gun down," I repeated. I sounded a lot calmer than I felt.

Anton made another grab for it, and the barrel swung wildly as Stanley pulled free. "Seriously, Anton, I *will* pistol-whip your crazy ass with this thing if you don't back off."

Anton did back up a few steps, but Stanley couldn't see the look on his face and keep an eye on me at the same time. If he had seen Anton's eyes go hard, I'm betting that I'm not the one he'd currently be aiming at. "You know who gets it all when they croak? Marnie." Stanley's voice shook. "I saw the will. They left everything to their fucking cook."

Anton reached into his overcoat.

I shook my head slowly, hoping that he would understand I meant for him not to do anything stupid. I think he got it. He paused.

"Maybe she'd been there longer than me, but so what? Who was the one covered in the old man's shit? Me. I deserved to be on that will, not her. So finally one day I'd had enough, and I told the old lady, right to her face—and what does she do? She fires me. And then that fat tub Gene came along, and within a month they'd called the lawyer, written him into the will."

"I'm not in anyone's will," I said. "I'm just the driver."

Stanley hefted the shotgun and peered through the sight. "I saw you walking in the yard with Edgar. You're already in tight with them. It's only a matter of time...." His finger squeezed the trigger, but Anton was quicker than he was. A long blade flashed as Stanley fired, and the shot went wide.

Most of the pellets that would've knocked a

hole in my skull blew past my shoulder, but a few of them clipped me, and between the force of the shot and the ice beneath my shoes, I went down. My ears rang, and my whole arm was numb, but I pried myself off the ground.

Anton and Stanley were down too. They grappled. A dark red trail of blood marked the frosted grass where they rolled. They struggled, and brighter red appeared—the vodka label, nested in a spray of glass shards that were nearly impossible to distinguish among the ice. I hoped the blood was all Stanley's.

Anton landed on top, probably because Stanley stopped struggling when the bowie knife was pressed into his throat. "I always thought you could be a real prick sometimes," said Anton, "but there was no one else around here to hang out with."

Stanley moved to sit up.

"I wouldn't, if I were you," said Anton. "Don't think my 'crazy ass' wouldn't love to cut you again."

"You wouldn't."

"You so sure about that?"

"Come on, man.... I think you really hurt me."

He sounded hurt, but I watched his hands tense and scrabble on the ground for a shard of glass he could use as a weapon. Anton was more difficult to read, but there was something in the set of his shoulders that made me think Stanley had appealed to his sympathy, and he was just about to cave in.

I crawled toward them and grabbed the shotgun. It was heavy, and it stank like a roll of caps that had just gotten a brick dropped on it. I knelt, held the stock, and pulled the pump. A spent casing popped out—the thing was huge—and another clunked into place. I staggered to my feet just as Stanley pulled an arm free and raised a shard of glass.

"Don't move." I leveled the muzzle at Stanley's eyes. The shotgun was a lot heavier than I thought it would be, but I didn't waver. My hands were steady...twenty-years-of-training steady. "Anton might not want to hurt you," I said, my voice low and cold, "but just give me a reason."

I held that damn gun until my arms ached, while Anton wrapped Stanley's arms together, then cut the twine from the ball with his bloody knife. The knife had glanced off Stanley's shoulder blade. The wound wasn't life threatening, but it bled a lot and probably hurt like a bitch.

Epilogue

"Is it going to hurt?" Anton asked me.

"I think you'll be able to handle it." I ran my fingers down the length of his bare thigh. I wanted to follow with my tongue, but it wouldn't be sanitary, nor would it be very professional of me. Not while the other artists and their customers were around, anyway.

The design he'd drawn on himself was strange, not exactly geometric, but not curvilinear either. "Are these supposed to be feathers?"

"Inspired by feathers. Or maybe ferns."

The proportion and flow were perfect. "How do you want them—solid? Shaded?"

"You're the pro. Collaborate with me."

I was the pro. Being with Anton, seeing him shift into his "zone" where nothing mattered but the things he created, made me realize that I might not miss owning a business, but I sorely missed doing tattoos. By the next time Mrs. White and I squared off again about hiring a nurse, I'd heard there was an empty chair in Mad Dog Martin's shop, and the choice seemed obvious.

I imagined Anton's design in delicate shades of gray, ephemeral, disappearing and reappearing as his quads flexed. I ran my hand down his leg again and pictured the design in vivid color, reds and yellows with intricate black outlines.

I glanced at his face. He lay on his stomach, hair spilling over his forearms, watching me, smiling. Pale skin, dark hair, dark eyes. I decided to go with black lines. Bold, like him.

I picked up the gauze in my left hand and the gun in my right and brushed the side of my hand over his thigh one more time. So smooth, even through the latex glove. "You only needed to shave the part I'm inking."

"Just being thorough."

I wondered how far up he'd shaved. His legs? His pubes? His whole body? It would itch like hell when it came back in, but for the next few days it would feel incredibly silky. I had no doubt that had been his intention. He was forever finding new ways to blow my mind. "You got any plans later?"

"Maybe."

I glanced at him. He was still watching me. Still smiling.

"Am I included in these plans?" I asked.

"Stop acting like you don't know what day it is."

"Sunday?"

Anton rolled his eyes and settled his head on his arm.

"I thought you didn't keep track of what day it was," I said.

"You've got a schedule. So it behooves me to know when I might have a shot at keeping you up all night."

"Maybe now you'll have some sympathy for my customers," I said. I spread my gloved fingers over his thigh. "Here goes." I inked a short line first, in case Anton turned out to be a flincher. He made a small noise in his throat, but he held still. A few drops of bloody ink oozed from the line. I dabbed it and inked another line.

"You really don't know?" he said. His voice was muffled by his sleeve.

"Hm?"

"Today. We've been together for six months. Half a year. A seventieth of a lifetime."

I inked a longer line, a graceful arc. I dabbed. "No—six months ago, we met. You didn't even touch me until two days later."

Anton considered that idea while the tattoo gun buzzed. I inked and blotted, inked and blotted, and a design began to take shape along the side of his thigh.

"Physically," he said, finally. "But mentally? I'd had you at least a hundred times by then."

"That's not a relationship. That's masturbation."

"I guess we'll have to agree to disagree."

We agreed to disagree a lot, usually over things much more serious than the official date of the start of our relationship. I was fine with it. I'd been with enough guys who were happy to lie to my face, then go behind my back and do the exact opposite of what they'd promised. I felt a lot safer with someone who had the balls to say what he meant. I ran my hand down Anton's leg again. He was pretty easy on the eyes too.

"And besides," he said, once he'd thought about it for a while. "If you're willing to shift some of your appointments around, we can celebrate through Wednesday, and then we'll both be right."

"Think so?" There were no appointments to shift. I hadn't set any, since I'd been hoping we could spend some time together, just the two of us. I didn't book myself solid anymore like I used to, and I'd grown accustomed to having some free time in my schedule, especially since I now had someone interesting to spend it with. Even if he sometimes stretched the boundaries of the word *interesting*. "You'll probably be climbing the walls by Wednesday."

"If we stay at your place, yeah. I was thinking something like...road trip."

"Like the time you called me from the U.P. with no money and an empty gas tank?"

"Um...not exactly. You can ration the gas money." Diane had seen fit to entrust Anton with a car, most likely to shut me up, because I can be a world-class nag when I set my mind to it. When I also cross my arms and give the "thug glare," as Anton calls it, I tend to get my way. Since I'd engineered Project Mobile Anton, I figured it was my responsibility to answer the occasional SOS. It was better than having him rely on me to get him off that island when he felt like stretching his legs. But that didn't mean I wouldn't tease him about it relentlessly.

I finished Anton's outline and stepped back for a look. I saw where the lines needed to be heavier and where I should shade. It was a sweet piece; we collaborated well.

"You want to see it so far?" I asked him.

"How close are we?"

"Another three, four hours of shading; then touch-ups once it's healed."

Anton settled his head on his crossed forearms. His glossy black hair trailed on the tabletop, and he watched me with one eye, its corner creased from him smiling. "Go for it, Ray of Moonlight. I don't need to see it. I trust you."

About this Story

Does each of us have a "type" we're attracted to? In some sense, sure. Ray isn't going to fall for some uptight preppy stock-trader any more than I'm going to decide a conservative football fan is my ideal mate. Not that anyone likes football in Wisconsin. (That would be a joke.)

I think what Ray is really worried about is that maybe he attracts the type of guy who can't be trusted and who only wants to use him. And I think that hard working, focused, type-A personalities really do tend to attract the sort of sponges who just see them as a comfortable, easy ride.

But in that sense, Anton is really the polar opposite of that little weasel, Johnny—and I think that's something Ray grows to realize by the end. True, Anton and Johnny are both terrible with money, and they both enjoy their recreational substances when they can lay their hands on them. But Anton is the most self-actualized person Ray will likely ever meet, and he's got so many engrossing ideas and ambitions, he doesn't need to fill a void inside of him by draining the hard work of his boyfriend.

Predictable? No. Anton will never be that. But being Anton's partner is invigorating enough to keep Ray from falling back into his workaholic patters, the ones that numbed him into avoiding his unhappiness and left him blind to his ex's manipulations.

I'm sad how it ended for the Whites—eventually they will need to figure out a more tenable solution to Mr.'s Alzheimer's. Things like dementia and bipolar don't simply go away. They can only be managed to lesser or greater success. I think that not being sucked into the Whites' drama was the healthiest thing Ray could have done for himself.

About the Author

Jordan Castillo Price was born and raised in the snow belt. She's had a healthy respect for the weather ever since her first car had an unfortunate encounter with a snowbank, and her high school homeroom friend needed to put his shoes on his hands to help her dig it out.

She currently owns a shiny red pair of snowshoes that even saw some action last winter. Though she can't say she's eager to break them out anytime soon.

Jordan is best known as the author of the PsyCop series, an unfolding tale of paranormal mystery and suspense starring Victor Bayne, a gay medium who's plagued by ghostly visitations. Also check out her mind-bending new series, Mnevermind, where memories are made...one client at a time.

Find out what's new at jordancastilloprice.com

More Stories

PSYCOP
1 Among the Living
1.1 Thaw
2 Criss Cross
2.1 Striking Sparks
2.2 Many Happy Returns
3 Body & Soul
3.1 Stroke of Midnight
3.2 Wood
4 Secrets
5 Camp Hell
6 GhosTV
6.1 In the Dark
6.2 Memento
7 Spook Squad

MNEVERMIND TRILOGY
1 Persistence of Memory
2 Forget Me Not
3 Life is Awesome

CHANNELING MORPHEUS

1 Payback
2 Vertigo
3 Manikin
4 Tainted
5 Rebirth
6 Brazen
7 Snare
8 Fluid
9 Swarm
10 Elixir
10.1 Jackpot
10.2 Canine

STANDALONE SHORTS & NOVELETTES

Betweentimes
Fire Thief
Sympathy
The Voice
Verdant

STANDALONE NOVELLAS & NOVELS

Body Art
Magic Mansion
Meatworks
Sleepwalker
The Starving Years
Turbulence Collection
Zero Hour: A Dystopian Adventure

www.ingramcontent.com/pod-product-compliance
Lightning Source LLC
Chambersburg PA
CBHW052143170626
46812CB00004B/1564